Books by Mollie Hunter
Available in HarperTrophy paperback editions

The Mermaid Summer

A Sound of Chariots

The Wicked One

Talent Is Not Enough
Mollie Hunter on Writing for Children

The Pied Piper Syndrome
And Other Essays

A
STRANGER
CAME
ASHORE

by Mollie Hunter

A Story of Suspense

 HarperTrophy®
A Division of HarperCollinsPublishers

Harper Trophy® is a registered trademark
of HarperCollins Publishers Inc.

LC Number 75-10814
ISBN 0-06-022651-X
ISBN 0-06-022652-8 (lib. bdg.)
ISBN 0-06-440082-4 (pbk.)
First Harper Trophy edition, 1977.

Nobody except a Shetlander *ever* gets it right, of course; but even so, this book is still for all my good friends in Shetland—especially Bruce and Freya Tulloch, and Maureen and Stuart Donald. And last—but very far from least—for Bobby (bucketing-about-in-a-small-boat) Tulloch.

M.H.

Contents

1

The Stranger

It was a while ago, in the days when they used to tell stories about creatures called the Selkie Folk.

A stranger came ashore to an island at that time—a man who gave his name as Finn Learson—and there was a mystery about him which had to do with these selkie creatures. Or so some people say, anyway; but to be exact about all this, you must first of all know that the Selkie Folk are the seals that live in the waters around the Shetland Islands. Also, the Shetlands themselves lie in the stormy seas to the north of Britain, and it was on a night of very fierce storm that it all began.

It so happened, then, that a ship named the *Bergen* was wrecked on one of the islands in this storm, and the shipwreck was near a place called Black Ness—which was not so much a place, really, as a scatter of houses on hilly ground overlooking the sea. Also, there was a certain Robbie Henderson living in

Black Ness at that time—a lad of twelve years old, according to all accounts—and he was the person most concerned in the mystery of this stranger, Finn Learson.

There were four other members of the Henderson family, however, apart from Robbie himself—his parents, Peter and Janet Henderson, his sister Elspeth, and his grandfather, Old Da Henderson. There was also the family's sheepdog, Tam; and as the storm grew wilder and wilder that night, this dog became very uneasy.

The whole family could hear how the storm was raging, of course, for their house stood close to the head of a long bay cutting into the rocky coast of the island—the kind of bay that Shetlanders call a "voe"—and so the thundering noise of the waves was very near. Even so, Old Da Henderson had the feeling that it was not just the storm that bothered Tam, for Old Da was pretty old and his head was simply full of the superstitions of those days. He listened, therefore: he waited, and he watched. And at last he noticed something which seemed to him the true cause of Tam's uneasiness.

"Look there!" said he, suddenly pointing to the fire of peats burning on the hearth.

The fire had been a good one, but now the peats at either side of it were burning down and crumbling into a fine white ash. A moment later there was only one of them left burning—the peat that stood upright at the center of the fire—and pointing again, Old Da went on,

"There! Do you see the way that peat has been left standing all by itself? That means a stranger will come here tonight!"

Peter Henderson cocked an ear to the noise of the wind howling over the thatch of the roof, and with a doubtful face on him he asked,

"What stranger could come to Black Ness *this* night?"

Old Da also turned an ear to the sound of the storm. "Well may you wonder about that," he said meaningly; and suddenly they all understood what he was thinking.

"A shipwreck in the voe!" Peter exclaimed, and was about to reach quickly for his jacket when there was a great thump, as if something heavy had fallen against the door of the house. The sound brought the whole family to its feet; and on that very instant the door burst wide open and a man came half staggering, half falling into the room.

Rain and wind swept in with him, raising a whirling cloud of peat ash from the fire. Peter rushed to the door, and threw all his burly weight on it to close it again. Robbie's mother and sister cried out, and clutched at one another. Robbie gripped hold of Tam, to stop him making a lunge at the stranger; and the stranger himself dropped to his knees on the floor, like a man completely exhausted.

As well he might be, the whole family realized when the struggle with the door was won and they had a chance to look properly at him. He had come straight out of the sea, it seemed, for he was streaming with water and he wore nothing except a pair of trousers held up by the kind of broad canvas money-belt that sailormen use. Moreover, there were strands of green seaweed plastered wetly to the skin of his bare back, and the hair that hung down from his drooping head was streaked with this same green weed.

"Poor fellow—oh, the poor fellow!" exclaimed Janet Henderson, gazing pitifully down on this, and then rushed to get a blanket to throw over him. Elspeth ran to fetch him a cup of hot tea. Robbie held grimly on to Tam, who was still snarling away at the crouching form; and Peter said in an awed voice,

"Well, you were right, Old Da. There's your stranger!"

"Aye, and you guessed rightly who it would be," Old Da returned. "This fellow *is* off a wreck. Just look at him—he must be!"

"No doubt of it," Peter agreed. Then, as Old Da moved to put fresh peats on the fire, he bent to touch the stranger's shoulder. "Who are you, lad?" he asked gently. "And where's your ship?"

The man began rising to his feet, looking about him in a dazed sort of way. He was young, they saw

4

then, a tall and powerfully built young man. Also, he was very handsome, with large and very dark-brown eyes. His hair was dark too—almost black, in fact; and, for all he was so young, it had streaks of a silvery-gray color across it.

"Who are you?" Peter asked again, but still taking care to make the question a gentle one; and slowly, in a deep, pleasant voice that had a foreign sort of sound to it, the young man answered,

"I call myself Finn—Finn Learson."

Tam began to snarl more fiercely than ever at that moment, and Robbie had to drag him even further away from the stranger. Janet came with the blanket to drape over his shoulders. Elspeth pressed the cup of tea into his hand. He smiled his thanks for all this, showing white and very even teeth that made him look more handsome than ever; and Peter asked once more,

"And your ship, lad? What about that? We'll get a boat out to her if we can, depend on it, for we are mostly seafaring men ourselves here."

Finn Learson sipped his tea, and then nodded in the direction of the voe. "The ship lies wrecked on the rocks down there," he said quietly. "But there is nothing you can do for her crew, for they are dead men now, all of them—swept away and drowned in the storm."

There was a little shocked silence at this. Then Old Da murmured,

"God rest their souls."

"Amen," the whole family responded; but by this time they had all noticed the foreign sound to Finn Learson's voice, and after another silence, Peter asked,

"Where was the ship from, then?"

"Ask that later," Janet put in firmly. "And meanwhile, it's time you got this young fellow into dry clothes."

"That sounds like sense," Peter admitted; and told Finn Learson, "Come on with me, and I'll let you have some of mine."

Off he went with this, into the room next door where all the family slept; for this was the way Shetland houses were built in those days, with only a living room called the but end, and a sleeping room called the ben end. Finn Learson followed Peter into the ben end, and Old Da decided,

"And I'll take a look down toward the voe, just in case it's possible to see the wreck from here."

"I'll come with you," offered Robbie, who was dying with curiosity about the wreck by this time.

The moment the two of them were outside the door, however, Robbie wished he had kept quiet; for the storm was on them, then, like a thousand wet, wild hands slapping from all directions. Moreover, for all there was only a short slope down to the voe, the night lay so black against their eyes that they could see nothing there except great fountains of spray bursting white against the darkness.

6

"It's no use!" Old Da shouted. "Wherever she is, a sea like that means the wreck is foundered by this time, anyway!"

They turned back into the house, their breath quite torn away by the storm; and as they struggled together to close the door, Old Da gasped,

"As for that Finn Learson, it's a miracle *he* managed to get ashore, for it would take the Selkie Folk themselves to stay alive in such a sea!"

"You're mad, the pair of you, going out into that storm," scolded Janet as they came shivering back to the fire. Then she turned to look at Finn Learson coming out of the ben room, dressed now in some of Peter's clothes, with his dark hair neatly combed and a pair of home-made sealskin shoes on his bare feet.

"That's better!" said she, and began bustling about to get everyone seated around the fire again.

Tam was still grumbling and growling, however, and so he had to be banished from the circle; but once that was done, Janet had peace to name the various members of the family to Finn Learson. Politely he nodded to each one in turn, but it was still on Elspeth Henderson that his great dark eyes came finally to rest—not that this surprised anyone, of course, since Elspeth had a fresh complexion and long, sandy-gold hair that made her just about the bonniest girl in the islands.

Elspeth was a bit shy of admiring looks, all the same, for she was only seventeen at that time. Besides which, she already had a young man of her own; and so, to spare her blushes under the stranger's gaze, Peter began quickly,

"Well, you're seemingly none the worse of your experience, my lad; and if you're ready to tell us, we're ready now to hear all about it."

Finn Learson gave a little shrug. "There is not much to tell," he remarked. "The ship was called the *Bergen*, and she was stoutly-enough built; but once she was caught in that north-west drift off the voe, there was no doubt she would drive on to the rocks there. And after that, there was no hope for her."

"The *Bergen* . . ." Peter echoed. "That sounds to me like a Norwegian name."

"There is a port in Norway called Bergen," Finn Learson agreed; and Peter went on,

"I suppose that accounts for the foreign sound to your voice, then. You'll be Norwegian yourself, are you?"

Finn Learson did not answer this in so many words, but he smiled in a way that seemed to mean this was indeed the case. And so, taking it for granted that he had guessed correctly, Peter remarked,

"All the same, you speak good English for a foreigner. I must say that for you!"

"Indeed he does," Janet agreed; but Finn Learson shook his head at this, and said modestly,

"I cannot take any credit for that. I have always been a great traveler, after all, and so I have had the chance to hear many languages."

8

"Well, you've had maybe the hardest voyage of your life this time," Old Da remarked, "for it beats me how *you* managed to get ashore when all the rest of the crew were drowned."

"They drowned because all the lifeboats were smashed and none of them could swim," Finn Learson explained. "But I have always been a strong swimmer—very strong. Moreover, I could see the light shining from your house, and so I knew I was not far from shore."

The thought of Old Da's remark about the Selkie Folk flashed across Robbie's mind, and he could not resist chiming in at this point,

"You were lucky, all the same!"

"Yes," Finn Learson agreed, and smiled a little. "Very lucky."

Now Robbie Henderson had what you might call a very noticing sort of mind, and there was something about this smile that struck him as being rather odd. The conversation was still going on, however; and so —even although this something had made him feel a bit uncomfortable—he had no time then to think why this should have been so.

2

Fiddle Music

It was to other shipwrecks at other times on the island that the talk had now turned, and after a while of this, Peter rose to take down a violin that was hanging on the wall.

"We're great folk to play the fiddle here, as maybe you've heard tell," he said to Finn Learson. "Indeed, there's hardly a house in these islands without a fiddle in it, and hardly a family without someone who can knock out a tune. But there's one tune we never play, except to mourn the death of one of our fisher lads. And so it's fitting now, it seems to me, that I should play it for your dead mates."

Tucking his fiddle under his chin then, Peter played the mourning song of the Shetland fishermen, and the rest of the family listened to it with tears not far away; for nothing can sing sweeter than a violin, and no music could have been sadder than this lament for drowned men. There was no telling what Finn

Learson thought of it, however, for he sat with one hand over his face all the time Peter was playing, and everyone had too much respect for his feelings to guess what expression he might be hiding.

Old Da was ready with the right words, nevertheless, once the music was finished and Peter was hanging the fiddle back in its place.

"That was well done, Peter," said he. "The souls of those poor fellows will rest easier for it; and as for their bodies, we will give them decent burial when the time comes."

Finn Learson looked up at these words. "How will you do that?" he asked curiously, and Old Da explained,

"Well, the bodies will drift ashore sooner or later, and then we'll bury them just above high-water mark at the place where they're found. For it's our custom, you know, never to take far from the sea anything the sea has claimed for its own."

"A wise custom," said Finn Learson, and smiled again, in the way that Robbie found rather odd. Then, with a glance at all the various bits of farming gear in the room, he asked,

"But you are farmers too, as well as fishermen, are you not?"

"You could say that, I suppose," Peter agreed. "Everybody here has the wee bit of land we call a 'croft'; and between that and the fishing, we manage to make *some* sort of a living."

"Och, Peter," Janet protested. "It's not such a bad living as all that!"

"No indeed. It's not all hard work for us here," Old Da assured Finn Learson. And with this to start it off, the talk was soon flowing with stories of life on the islands, for the but end was now all set for this kind of talk.

The fire was red and cheerful. The only other light in the room was the gentle glow from a little lamp filled with fish-oil—a "kollie," as it was called. Moreover, the hour was just right for story-telling, and Finn Learson was always ready with a question of the kind that would start yet another story.

So the time ran on that night without any of the Hendersons realizing how neatly all these questions were putting a stop to the ones they might have been asking *him*. The grandfather clock in the but end chimed midnight. Everyone suddenly realized how late it was; and with her eyes on the clock, Janet reminded them,

"We have an early rise tomorrow."

The rest of the family knew what she meant by this, for those were hard times when the salvage off a wreck was precious, and they would all have to be down early at the voe to get what they could from the *Bergen*. They took the hint to rise, therefore, and Janet waved Finn Learson toward the wooden settle standing against one wall of the room.

"You can take that blanket I gave you and sleep

there, on the restin' chair," said she, and then steered Elspeth ahead of her into the ben room.

Old Da followed in a minute or so. Robbie and Peter stayed to bank down the fire for the night and to put out the kollie; and it was then, with his fingers reaching up to close on the wick of the kollie, that Robbie noticed Tam creeping back to his usual place by the fire.

"You'll not mind old Tam, will you?" he asked. "He's not fierce, really—just a bit upset by everything tonight."

Finn Learson stretched out on the restin' chair and pulled the blanket close around himself. One eye gleamed at Robbie over the edge of this blanket—a bright, and somehow very watchful eye. A voice came, muffled by the blanket's folds.

"Off you go, lad," said the voice. "I'll know how to calm your dog if it snarls again."

Still Robbie hesitated, for there was something he did not like about the tone of the muffled voice. His father only laughed at it, however, and reached over Robbie's head to snuff out the kollie.

"Aye, surely," he agreed as he did this. Then, with a good-night to Finn Learson from both him and Robbie, they too went ben to their beds.

They were proper old-fashioned Shetland beds, these, made like a large box complete with a lid on top and a sliding door in one side. There were air-holes in the sliding doors, neatly pierced in the shapes

13

of hearts and diamonds; the box beds themselves stood on legs that raised them above drafts, and there were three of them in the room—one for Peter and Janet, one for Elspeth, and one that Robbie shared with Old Da.

Robbie was dead tired by this time, and he lost not a moment in getting in beside Old Da. Almost instantly then, he was asleep, for the bed was comfortable and Old Da had warmed it for him. But just as suddenly, it seemed to him, he was awake again, wondering how long he had slept and what had happened to wake him.

There was no sound or movement in the ben room, he realized. But there *was* a sound coming from somewhere—the sound of a fiddle very softly played and near at hand—and for several startled moments he lay wondering who on earth could be playing the fiddle at that hour of night.

Robbie's surprise was soon over, however, and it was uneasiness that gripped him then; for by the end of those first few moments he had realized that the music was coming from the but end of the house where his father's fiddle hung. And yet his father was lying asleep in the box bed a few feet away from his own! The sliding door of this bed was open, and he could see his father there—which meant that the only person who could be playing the fiddle was the stranger, Finn Learson. And why should *he* be doing that at such an hour?

14

Moreover, Robbie thought, there was something very odd about the music itself, something very eerie and mysterious, for there was no tune to it—or nothing he could recognize as a tune, at least. It was just like voices sliding up and down a scale, in fact; high voices, echoing very sad and sweet in some hollow place, and in spite of the warmth of the bed, the sound they made was beginning to send shivers up and down his back.

Crouching lower into the warmth, Robbie tried not to hear the voices; but he was curious about them, as well as uneasy. Besides which, he told himself, that Finn Learson had no *right* to be playing his Da's fiddle, and he had a good mind to say so to his very face! This was the very thought to give his curiosity the spur it needed, and gaining courage from it, he slipped cautiously out of bed.

A draft of cold air blew around his bare legs. The floor of the ben room was cold too, for it was only beaten earth, hard-packed and polished from the use of many years. With his toes curling away from the feel of this floor, Robbie padded to the door of the ben room. For a moment he stood there, shivering as much from the cold now as from uneasiness. Then, carefully, he advanced a hand to the doorknob.

The noise of Tam growling began to sound through the music; and instantly on this, it stopped. Tam's growls grew louder, then began to die again; and tightening his grasp on the knob, Robbie pulled the door open far enough to allow him to see into the but end.

It was a roomful of strange shapes and shadows that met his eye, for the fire was still sending out a red glow that lit some things and left others in darkness. Even so, he saw that his father's fiddle was gone from its usual place on the wall, and there was no form stretched out under the blanket on the restin' chair. The fiddle now lay on top of this blanket, as if Finn Learson had hurriedly placed it there; and Finn Learson himself was kneeling on one knee in front of the fire, with Tam crouching in front of him.

The dog's back was towards Robbie, but both dog and man were lit by the fire's glow, and Robbie saw that Finn Learson had his hands cupped lightly around Tam's head. His eyes were fixed on Tam's eyes, and it seemed to Robbie that he was commanding Tam to silence with this stare.

It struck Robbie, too, that Tam was afraid of the look holding him there as well as fascinated by it, for the dog was shivering all over its body. Lower and lower it crouched, its eyes never leaving Finn Learson's eyes, its growl fading with every second of the look; until finally, it was altogether silent.

Finn Learson drew his hands away from its head, and in that same moment he looked up, straight into Robbie's eyes. The firelight fell on his face, making a gleaming red mask of it in the surrounding dusk. His great dark eyes seemed bigger and darker than ever in that red mask, and the effect of all this sent a stab of fear through Robbie.

Everything he had meant to say fled from his mind then, and all he could think of was getting back to his safe, warm bed. Stepping backwards he began gently to close the door, and as he did so, Finn Learson rose to his feet. Robbie's heart quickened its beat still further, but he continued with his gentle closing of the door; and the last thing he saw in the last inch of its closing was Tam, still staring up in fascination at the man in front of him.

Quickly and silently then, Robbie dashed for his bed, and creeping into it, he lay wondering about everything that had happened. It was very late at night by this time, however, and he was still tired. Also, it was very cozy, lying there in the warmth beside Old Da. Robbie soon found he was too drowsy to think properly; and promising himself he would work out all the whys and wherefores of it in the morning, he drifted off to sleep again.

3

Gold . . .

The storm had not quite blown itself out by the time morning came, and the Hendersons woke to find that Old Da had been right in thinking the *Bergen* had foundered. There was plenty of wreckage from it, however, and this was already drawing people down from all the other houses on the hill overlooking the voe.

"Come on!" urged Janet, giving everyone breakfast on the run; but Robbie had something more than wreckage to think about at that moment, for strange events that happen in the middle of the night have a way of seeming as far off and unreal as a dream the next day, and this was how things were for him then.

He stared around the but end, wondering if he had indeed dreamt the events of the night before; for there was his father's fiddle hanging in its usual place, and there was Tam dozing peacefully as usual in front of the fire. There was Finn Learson too, looking like any other young man supping porridge along with everyone else, and not giving a single hint or sign that he had ever moved from his night's sleep on the restin' chair.

Robbie swallowed down his own porridge, telling himself that he *must* have dreamt about the strange music and the look that had commanded Tam to silence. It was impossible to imagine otherwise, in fact, with everything now so much as usual and daylight making the but end itself seem such an ordinary place!

The need to make haste in starting the salvage work began to take a grip on him also, so that even the "dream" grew fainter in his mind. Then came something else which drove it still further away. A voice called from outside the house, the familiar and very cheerful voice of Elspeth's young man, Nicol Anderson; and Nicol, as it happened, was also Robbie's very good friend.

Robbie rushed to let him in to the but end, and then the place seemed crowded, for Nicol was a big fellow—as big and powerful a man as Finn Learson, in fact. Moreover, he had gleaming red hair that gave him the look of a big, smiling sun when he laughed, and which also drew even more attention to his height.

"Who's ready to come down to the voe, then?" he asked, after all the explanations about Finn Learson had been made; and instantly, Robbie was on his feet.

"I am!" said he. Then off he hurried to the voe

with Nicol, firmly putting even the memory of his strange "dream" from his mind, and never thinking he was making the great mistake of his young life in doing so.

Robbie was in good company with this, however, for everyone else in Black Ness made mistakes that morning; and naturally enough, these were the same ones that the Henderson family had already made about Finn Learson.

No one doubted for a moment that he was indeed a survivor of the wreck, and so there was nothing but sympathy for him. No one asked him any more questions than had already been asked—there was no time for this, since the wreckage was so widely scattered over the voe that everyone was anxious to get it ashore before it could drift even further. Moreover, Finn Learson immediately offered his help in this work; and since Nicol Anderson was the only man there who equaled him in size and strength, this offer was eagerly accepted.

So, for hours after that, the work went on, with Finn Learson bending his back so willingly to it that there was even greater sympathy for him when the tide eventually brought the bodies of the *Bergen*'s crew washing ashore.

Old Da Henderson was as good as his word, however, and the bodies were buried just above high-water mark at the point where they were found. A stone was placed to mark each grave, a hymn was sung, and Old Da spoke a prayer.

"Amen," said everyone at the end of this. And that "*Amen*" was the final word on the wreck of the *Bergen*; for, the way they all saw it then, it was bad enough for a young fellow like Finn Learson to lose all his mates in one night without folk asking questions that would only remind him of this loss.

There was still the question of what he would do next, however; and so, after supper that night, Peter began,

"And what are your plans now, lad? Are you thinking of going back to your own country?"

"No," said Finn Learson, taking a sideways glance at the fiddle on the wall. "I'm in no hurry to do that."

"Then what will you do?" Peter asked. "Will you take ship for another voyage?"

"Indeed no!" Finn Learson told him. "It's the land for me for a while."

"And no one could blame you for that!" Peter agreed. "Which means you'll be here for a few days yet, I suppose—and welcome, I'm sure, if you do not mind our sort of life."

"Far from that," Finn Learson assured him. "I think it must be a fine life! A few weeks of it, in fact—or even a few months—would be nearer what I have in mind."

Now the Hendersons were hospitable people, but they were also much too poor to be burdened for months with a pair of idle hands and an idle mouth to feed. Yet where was Finn Learson to live if he stayed for months on the island, unless it was with them? None of them had the answer to this question, but Finn Learson guessed the meaning of their silence, and quickly he added,

"But I would not expect to stay here for nothing, of course!"

With his hand reaching into the pouch of his canvas money-belt as he said this, he pulled out a coin and laid it on the table; but this only left the Hendersons even more lost for words, for the coin was a large one and it was made of gold. It was also an old coin, so old that the pattern had been rubbed almost smooth; and as they stared in wonder at it, Finn Learson asked anxiously,

"Is that not enough?"

"Enough!" Janet exclaimed. "It's a fortune, man! But where in the world did you get so ancient a coin?"

"Off a sunken treasure ship!" guessed Robbie, thinking that this must certainly be the answer; but his father frowned, and told him,

"You talk an awful lot of nonsense, boy."

"I don't know about that," Old Da objected. "I remember, when I was a young man I saw a coin washed ashore from a Spanish treasure ship that was wrecked in ancient times on this island. A piece of eight, they called it, and it looked exactly like this one."

"I don't doubt you," Peter remarked. "But you

know what Robbie is like! He was letting his fancy run away with a whole shipload of treasure, instead of the odd piece a sailorman might pick up on his travels—which is where this one came from, I'll wager!"

Finn Learson smiled at this—the same, rather odd little smile Robbie had noticed the night before. "Yes, of course," he agreed. "It *is* just something I picked up on my travels. And since I have no coins in my belt of the kind you use, it is all I can offer you."

"But we cannot take it," Janet declared, "for gold does not lose its value however old the coins that are made from it. And this one is worth more than it would cost to keep you, supposing you stayed for a year with us."

Finn Learson began to speak again, but Peter checked him. "Wait," said he. "Let me tell you this. There is no money to be made from fishing in the voe, and none either from working a croft. And so, all the men like myself have to go off every summer to earn money at the deep-sea fishing—the *haaf*, as we call it. But before we can do that, there is all the spring work of the croft to be tackled—digging, planting, sowing, cutting peats—"

"I see what's in your mind!" Old Da interrupted, and then turned ruefully to Finn Learson. "I'm getting too old to share such hard work," he went on, "and Robbie is still too young to give a man's help on the croft. Yet there are only six weeks left now before Peter goes off to the *haaf*, and if he does not manage to get the crops in before then, how will we all eat next winter?"

"But if you were willing to help me with that work," Peter finished, "it would be worth more to us than the cost of your stay here, and it would give you a real chance to try our kind of life. So, what do you say, Finn Learson?"

"I say 'done!'" Finn Learson exclaimed. "But you must still have the gold, for it may still cost you more than you think to have me here."

"Nonsense!" Peter and Janet protested together, and Peter began sliding the coin across the table to Finn Learson. Yet still he would not allow this.

"If you will not take it in payment," said he, "take it at least as a keepsake of me when I have gone back to my own country."

Firmly he pushed the coin back across the table. Then, with a glance at Elspeth, he added,

"There! When you look at that, you'll remember it did not seem half so bright to me as the gold of your daughter's hair."

Elspeth blushed scarlet at this, but the others laughed at such a compliment.

"Would you not like Nicol to say fine things like that?" Robbie teased her; and Peter told Finn Learson,

"Well, we can hardly refuse it on *those* terms!"

And so it was settled. Elspeth stood the coin on its edge like an ornament on the mantlepiece; and there it stayed, its smooth surface glittering in the light of the kollie. Janet made up a proper bed for Finn Learson in the barn that was built onto the gable wall of the but end; and he also stayed, to help Peter with all the work that had to be done before the *haaf*.

4

. . . and Dancing and Gold

The new arrangement, it seemed, was going to be a good one—and not just for Peter, either.

The whole family felt the benefit of it, for Robbie and Old Da had now more time each day to go fishing in the voe, and a good catch of fish meant more food for everyone. Also, they had more time to look after the livestock, and so there were fewer lambs and calves lost than in any year before that. Moreover, Finn Learson himself settled down so quickly that he was no trouble at all to anyone—quite the opposite, in fact.

He worked hard, yet still he continued so polite and pleasant in his ways that both Janet and Elspeth were quite taken by his charm and declared he was a pleasure to have around. Peter was delighted to have such a strong and willing helper. Tam no longer barked or growled at him; so that, in no time at all it seemed, he was coming and going about the place as if he had always lived there.

"He's a silent sort of man, though, isn't he?" Old Da remarked one day to Janet. "A good listener, mark you—indeed, I've never seen a man for watching and listening so closely to everything that goes on. Yet he never has much to say on his own account."

"That's no great fault!" Janet exclaimed. "And one talker in the house is enough, surely?"

Old Da laughed. "Now you're having a dig at me," he teased Janet, for it was perfectly true that Old Da was a great talker; and although they were all glad enough of his stories around the fire in the wintertime, Janet and Peter were inclined to complain that Robbie took all this kind of talk too seriously. *"Letting his imagination run away with him,"* they called it; which was a foolish habit, in their opinion, and therefore one which should be checked before it got too strong a grip on him.

This was not to the point at that moment, however, and so Janet simply ignored Old Da's teasing. "Anyway," she finished, "the main thing is that Finn Learson is settling here as to the manner born, and that should be enough for all of us."

So the Hendersons went on talking from time to time among themselves about the new arrangement —all except Robbie, that is, for no one thought of asking *his* opinion. Moreover, he would not have known what to answer even if he had been asked, for Finn Learson was still given to smiling that odd little smile he had worn first on the night of the storm, and Robbie did not care for this.

27

It was like someone smiling at a secret joke, he thought, and felt uneasy at such an idea. On the other hand, there was no doubt that Finn Learson had a powerful charm of manner which made him *want* to like the man. . . .

So Robbie swithered and swayed in the opinion that was never asked, and meanwhile, Finn Learson was getting acquainted with all the rest of the people in Black Ness. Very easy he found this, too, for all that he was a man of few words, since there is nothing Shetlanders enjoy better than visiting back and forward in one another's houses.

Sooner or later also, on such occasions, out will come the fiddle. All the young folk—and very often some of those that are not so young—will get up to have a dance; and the first evening that this was the way of things in the Hendersons' house, Finn Learson showed the lightest, neatest foot in the whole company.

He was merry as a grig, too, clapping his hands in time to the fiddling, white teeth flashing all the time in a laugh, eyes glittering like two great dark fires in his handsome head. No amount of leaping and whirling seemed to tire him, either; and curiously looking on at this with Robbie and Janet, Old Da remarked,

"Well, there's one stranger that knows how to make himself at home on the islands!"

"Indeed, aye," Janet agreed, admiring the light

footwork that was going on. "A man who can dance like that is sure of a welcome in Black Ness."

And so it turned out, of course, for a good dancer is always a challenge to the skill of a good fiddler. Moreover, a handsome young man who is also neat and light on his feet is a catch for any girl; and the result of all this was that Finn Learson soon found himself welcome anywhere the young folk were trying to stir things up for a bit of a dance.

No one minded, either, that he had so little to say for himself. He was a foreigner, after all, they excused him; and he could hardly be expected to chatter in a tongue that was strange to him. Occasionally too, when it struck someone that there was a certain oddness in the intent way he listened and watched in other folks' company, this was also put down to the fact that he was a stranger to the islands, and therefore curious about life there.

There was one person in Black Ness, however, who was not too pleased to see him staying on with the Hendersons, and that was Elspeth's young man, Nicol Anderson. This was just natural jealousy on his part, of course, Finn Learson being so handsome and Elspeth so young and bonny. But after all, as Peter took care to point out to Nicol, it was only until the spring work was finished; and once that was the case, there was no doubt Finn Learson would return to his own country.

About a week before the start of the *haaf* season,

however, Peter found himself thinking differently, for it was then that one of his boat's crew fell sick. There was not a man in Black Ness to replace him, either; and so, after thinking all around the subject, Peter said to Finn Learson,

"It's like this, you see. It's a boat called a 'sixareen' we use at the *haaf*, because it takes six men to row it. Yet here I am now, one short of my crew; and even with strong young fellows like Nicol Anderson among them, a sixareen is a heavy craft to pull. And so I'm in trouble, unless— Unless, maybe, *you* would be willing to make up my crew for me."

Finn Learson shook his head at this. "The kind of deep-sea fishing I have learned," said he, "is not likely to be the kind you practice."

"Och, we'll soon take care of that!" Peter exclaimed. "We'll teach you all you need to know. And just think of the money you could make at the *haaf*! Besides which, you would very likely enjoy it for its own sake, for it's out there in the deep water where the big fish lie that you get the real fishing and the real feel of the sea!"

"*Out there in the deep water . . .*" Finn Learson repeated softly, his eyes beginning to gleam with the excitement that lit them when he was dancing. He was silent for a moment, with everyone waiting expectantly for his next word, then suddenly he decided.

"I *would* enjoy that," he told Peter. "To be out there in the deep water with the sea all around me again—that would be fine. I'll go with you to the *haaf*!"

So that was another matter settled, and the night before Peter and his crew left for the fishing station in the north of the islands, they all met for a celebration in the Hendersons' house. Peter filled glasses for everyone to drink a toast, but before he could utter one word of this, Nicol Anderson said,

"Hold on, Peter. What toast are you going to give?"

Peter stared at him. "The usual one, of course," he said. "The one we always drink before we go to the *haaf*."

"Aye, I thought so," Nicol answered. "But if that is the way of it, we cannot have a man in the boat who does not even know the meaning of the toast. And so, before Finn Learson comes with us, he must first guess the answer to a riddle."

Everyone began to smile at this, guessing riddles being a favorite game in Shetland. Nicol seemed to be in deadly earnest, however, which made the Hendersons realize that there was a bit of rivalry building up now between the two young men. Yet still, Peter realized, Nicol had every right to put out such a challenge. And so, even although he could see himself being short of a crew member at the very last moment, he had to allow it.

"On you go, then," said he; and staring Finn Learson right in the eye, Nicol said,

"Right—read me this riddle, Finn Learson. *What head is it that wears no hair?*"

Now this was such a very old Shetland riddle that no one outside the islands could possibly guess the meaning of it. Or so everyone thought, anyway; yet even so, Finn Learson took only a moment to think before he answered,

"There's no hair on the head of a fish; and so that is the reading of your riddle—the fish!"

There was a burst of applause at this. Even Nicol applauded, for he was most certainly not the kind of man to hold on to ill-feeling. Moreover, Finn Learson had spoken in the most friendly and pleasant way, and so now Nicol answered him with his usual big sun-burst of a smile.

"You've earned your place in the boat," he agreed, and then turned to tell Peter, "Give your toast, man!"

"I will that!" exclaimed Peter, relieved at this pleasant outcome of an awkward moment. Then, raising his glass high, he shouted,

"Here we go then, boys. It's off to the *haaf*, and 'Death to the head that wears no hair!' "

"Death to the head that wears no hair!" the whole crew echoed, shouting; and drained their glasses on the words.

"And a tune or two before the night is out!" added

Peter, reaching for his fiddle and starting up a reel.

So the celebration began for everyone except Robbie, who was still puzzling over the way Finn Learson had solved the riddle; and under cover of all the noise, he said to Old Da,

"There's no one outside the islands has ever managed to read that riddle, Old Da. And so how did *he* guess the answer?"

Now Old Da had been forming his own idea about this, just as he had slowly been forming ideas about other matters concerning Finn Learson—particularly those of the gold coin he had brought ashore, and also his love of dancing. Old Da's thoughts on such matters, however, were all very sober ones which he had no intention of telling to anyone at the moment. Least of all did he mean to tell them to Robbie; and so now he got out of the situation by saying,

"Maybe he already knew the answer to it, Robbie. Or maybe he guessed it just because he's a clever man."

"Aye, maybe," Robbie agreed; but he was not satisfied with this, and he went to his bed still puzzling over it.

The next day when all the men had gone to the *haaf*, he was still thinking about it; and this kept his eyes going to the only reminder of Finn Learson that was now left in the house—the gold coin on the mantelpiece.

Finn Learson had never actually denied that it had

come from a sunken treasure-ship, he told himself. And so, where and how it had been picked up on his travels was still a mystery. Moreover, Finn Learson himself was still a mystery, for no one knew a thing more about him than they had when he first arrived on the island. And that was six weeks ago, Robbie thought; which did indeed make him a clever man—much more clever, in fact, than anyone except himself seemed to have realized!

There was his smile, too—that strange little smile which made him look as if he had some secret to hide. . . .

Robbie stared at the coin as if staring by itself could tell him how Finn Learson had come by it. But the more he stared, the less he could think of an answer to this, and the more the coin seemed to wink back at him like an ancient golden eye that had its own secret to keep.

5

The Selkie Summer

There was little to do on the croft once the men had gone, but Robbie and Old Da were still kept busy in various ways.

The eggs and young of seabirds were in season, and these were needed to provide something extra for the pot. The different kinds of moss that Janet and Elspeth used for dyeing cloth had also to be picked at that time of the year; and of course, there was always fishing to be done. It happened to be an unusually fine summer that year, however, so that Robbie and Old Da were soon having a high old time to themselves.

For days at a time the weather held. The sun made the grass look greener than green, the sky bluer than blue, and the two of them chose the finest of these fine days to get their bag of eggs and young seabirds. Not that they were intent simply on getting the best of the weather on these occasions, mind you, for it was on the ledges of the high cliffs above the voe that the seabirds nested, and Robbie could easily have been blown into the sea if he had tried scrambling down there on windy days.

With Old Da to guide him, however, Robbie never made any such mistake. He always climbed barefoot, too, which helped to give his toes a grip on the steep rock face; and since he had a good head for heights, he enjoyed all this scrambling about the cliffs. As for Old Da, he had done the very same climbs in his own young days; and so he was in his glory now, leaning over the clifftop to shout advice and encouragement on each one that Robbie attempted.

Gathering moss for dyes was another ploy for the finest weather, for then Old Da would take Robbie and Tam on a whole day of wandering footloose among the hills where such moss was to be found. To Robbie's great pleasure too, as they wandered like this, Old Da told him one story after another, and there was only one thing that could cast a gloom on such a day.

It was always Tam who gave warning of such a gloom, too, and it always happened in the same way. Tam would start to whine, and then the other two would realize they were approaching a sort of long, shadowy hollow where no flowers grew; and here and there, in such hollows they would see a green mound with a door hole that was screened by ferns.

"Aye, the dog has a sixth sense about such places," Old Da would interrupt himself to say then, and they would all hurry past the hollow; for these green mounds were said to be the homes of a small people called *trows*. And trows are creatures of the Otherworld which is not human.

Once they were clear of such places, however, the feeling of gloom lifted from them, and Old Da would go on with his story-telling. Yet still he kept his voice low, for now his stories would be about the trows themselves, and these are creatures that are quick to take offense at anything said about them. Moreover, trows can make themselves invisible at will, and trowie ears are sharp ears!

"Have you ever seen a trow?" Robbie sometimes asked. But Old Da would not answer yes or no to this, and so Robbie had to be content with listening, and wondering, and keeping a sharp lookout on his own account.

Mornings and evenings of every day were the times when the two of them went fishing, sometimes casting their lines from the clifftop, and sometimes rowing out in the small boat that was kept for this purpose; but it was the boat-trips Robbie preferred, for there were always seals swimming in the voe, and this gave him the chance to follow his liking for watching these creatures at close quarters.

The interest in seals was something else he had learned from Old Da, of course; for Old Da had long ago taught him the trick of holding the boat so steady in one place that they lost all fear of it. Little, feathery strokes of the oars were the secret of this trick, and as soon as Robbie had mastered this way of "feathering" with the oars, he found the seals swimming quite close to the boat and surfacing on all sides of it.

"They like music," Old Da told him then; and to prove this, he began to sing. Immediately the seals reared chest-high out of the water to stare towards the sound of his voice, and Old Da laughed to see this.

"I told you," he remarked. "And now I'll tell you something else about the Selkie Folk and music. They have a great envy of the way people like ourselves can dance to it; and so they gather sometimes on a lonely beach where they can cast off their skins and take human form. And there they sing, and dance to the music of this singing."

Robbie stared at this, for neither he nor anyone else could ever be sure how much was true in Old Da's stories, and how much was made up. He was still curious to know more about the Selkie dancing, however, and so he asked,

"But *how* can they cast off their skins and change like that?"

"You'll have to put that question to a wiser man than me," Old Da told him, "for the only answer I can give you is that selkies are a lot more than they seem to be. They are not animal creatures at all, in fact, but a kind of folk that have been doomed to live as selkies—a strange, gifted folk, who have powers *we* do not understand."

Robbie considered this, still feeling a bit doubtful. "What kind of folk?" he asked. And solemnly, Old Da answered,

"Fallen angels. Angels that sinned against Heaven, when Heaven was shining new; and for their sins, were cast out from all that glory."

"Oh!" said Robbie, feeling a shiver run up his back at this. "Oh, my!" And he shivered again, still not knowing what to believe, for it was hard to think of all these inquisitive creatures around the boat as fallen angels. And yet, when he looked at the wise, and somehow sad expression of their great dark eyes, he was more than half persuaded that Old Da was speaking truly after all.

"You're forgetting to feather," Old Da reminded him; which was true. And what with the way this had allowed the boat to rock, the seals were all beginning to dive out of sight.

Old Da chuckled to see them scatter like this, and began to sing again in his quavery, old man's voice,

"*I am a man upon the land,*
A selkie in the sea—"

"What's that song?" interrupted Robbie.

"An old one, that tells about the Great Selkie," said Old Da; but of course, this only brought another question from Robbie.

"Who's the Great Selkie?" he wanted to know then, and Old Da told him,

"Ah, well now. That's another story, Robbie! He's the King of all the selkies, he is; which means he's the great bull seal that has his home deep, deep down in the deepest sea. That's where the selkies' own country is; and that's where he rules, from a palace that has walls of crystal and floors of coral, with sea anemones for jewels, and a roof of waving golden weed. Or maybe the roof is made of waving golden hair—the hair of drowned girls. Nobody knows for sure, for people can enter that country, but they cannot come back again."

"Why not?" asked Robbie, staring fascinated at Old Da. "Why can they not come back?"

"Because the Great Selkie will not allow it," Old Da told him.

"And the drowned girls?" Robbie asked. "Who were they?"

"Well," said Old Da thoughtfully, "they do say that every now and then this Great Selkie manages to tempt some poor lass to enter his kingdom. And when she tries to escape back to her own kind—as she must sooner or later always want to do—that is what happens to her."

"I don't believe that," declared Robbie, deciding

that Old Da was just making it up after all; but Old Da just laughed at this, and went on with another story.

All this was long before that particular summer, however, and most of Old Da's stories were dim in Robbie's mind by then. He was not a bit less interested in the selkies themselves, all the same, and so Old Da patiently taught him a little more each day about the true life of these creatures.

"You know how they come ashore each year when their pups are due to be born," said he, on one of these occasions. "Well, believe it or not, Robbie, these same pups are all four weeks old before they even start learning to swim. Yet, for all that, they still grow up to be the most traveled of any sea-creatures."

"Where do they go?" Robbie asked curiously.

"Out into the Atlantic Ocean," Old Da told him. "And if they are bull selkies, they spend the whole of the first seven or eight years of their lives wandering all the seas of the world before they come back here to rejoin their own kind."

Robbie sat watching the fishing lines they had cast, and thinking of all the selkie pups he had seen. They were such helpless little creatures, he remembered; and it was strange, very strange, to think of them growing up to be so adventurous.

"We'll go and have a look at this year's pups, will we?" he asked, and Old Da agreed,

"Of course, Robbie. Come September or October when the pups are born, we'll go off as usual and watch them to your heart's content."

And maybe then, Robbie thought secretly, he would get to do at last what he had always wanted to do—pick up one of the pups and hold it so that he could discover what a seal *felt* like. Old Da guessed what he was thinking, however, and said sternly,

"But you're not to try touching them, mind! You'll only get a bite from their sharp little teeth, if you do that."

"Who said I wanted to touch them?" protested Robbie, trying to look innocent. "And anyway, you'll not get *me* risking a walk into a nursery of selkie pups with two or three of those great, powerful bull selkies roaring away in the middle of it!"

"Now that's wise," Old Da remarked approvingly, and went on to talk of how he had learned about seals in his own young days.

So, in this way, Robbie managed to add quite a bit that summer to the store of information he already had about selkies; and when the menfolk came home for a weekend from the fishing station—which they occasionally did throughout the *haaf* season—he began boasting to his father of all he had learned.

"Well," remarked Peter after a while of patient listening to this, "I'm glad to know your Old Da is telling you useful things nowadays, as well as all those fanciful tales of his."

Old Da chuckled at this remark. Then he turned to Finn Learson, who had also been listening; and with his face growing serious again, he asked,

"And what do *you* think I should tell Robbie about selkies?"

Finn Learson smiled the little smile that made him look as if he were enjoying some secret joke.

"I think," said he drily, "that you should tell him exactly as much as you think proper for him to know, for I also think that you are a very wise old man."

"And you could be right at that," remarked Old Da, looking hard at him.

Robbie stared at them both, wondering what lay behind this peculiar scrap of conversation; but nobody else seemed to notice anything unusual about it, and the weekend was so very quickly over that he had no time to ponder it as he would have liked.

Very shortly after that particular weekend, also, something else happened which put every other thought completely out of his mind. Old Da fell ill —very ill. And after a time it looked as if he would die.

6

Old Da's Warning

There was nothing much wrong with Old Da at first
—just a chill that he took after getting his feet wet
one day; but it was soon plain that he could not
throw off this chill, and Janet altered the sleeping
arrangements so that he would have more room to
toss and turn at night.

Elspeth, she decided, would move in beside herself,
while Robbie took Elspeth's bed; yet even when
this was done and Old Da had a bed to himself, he
still could not get a peaceful night's sleep. His bones
shook with the fever that was on him, his breath
came hard and painful. Watching him, Janet feared
for the worst; and quietly, without telling the young
people what she was about, she sent word to Peter of
his condition.

Each night after that she lay awake for a long time,
uneasily listening to the way the old man's breath
wheezed and rattled in his chest. Through the day,

Robbie and Elspeth took turns to sit with him; but it was Robbie's company he liked best, and it was while he sat by the box bed holding the hot, paper-thin old hand between his own strong young hands, that Robbie at last also realized his Old Da was dying.

This was a hard fact to face; and what made it harder was that Old Da seemed so anxious to talk to him, yet still could do no more than wheeze out a few words at a time. Robbie kept telling him to rest, not to bother talking; but still Old Da persisted, as if what he had to say was important—even urgent—and Robbie got the strangest feeling that he was trying to utter a warning of some kind.

For two days this went on. Then, on the evening of the second day, Old Da said in a clear and perfectly normal voice,

"Robbie, listen to me."

Robbie saw that his eyes were wide open, and quite calm. He waited for the next word, and Old Da said,

"I should have told you all before this, but I wasn't sure. Now I'm dying, and I *must* speak. Don't trust him, Robbie. *Don't trust him.*"

"Trust who?" asked Robbie, bewildered by this; and with his voice getting fainter now, Old Da answered,

"Finn Learson."

"But why not?" Robbie demanded. "You've got

to have a reason for saying that, Old Da. Why shouldn't I trust him?"

Old Da struggled to sit up. "This is the reason," he began. "It has to do with gold, Robbie, and dancing, and the crystal palace under the sea—"

Old Da's breath was wheezing painfully again, and Robbie was alarmed by this. It seemed to him too, that the old man was now talking very strangely, and so he said quickly,

"I'll call my Mam."

"No—my breath is going!" exclaimed Old Da, clutching at him. "Listen first, then tell the others. Tell Elspeth. She's the one in danger—"

"*Mam!*" interrupted Robbie, shouting, for he was in real fear now over the way Old Da was panting. "Come quick, Mam!"

"It has happened before," Old Da's wheezing voice persisted faintly. "Listen, Robbie. There was another stranger like Finn Learson. He came ashore the way Finn Learson did, and the story about him was that he . . ."

Old Da's voice faded to nothing. He made a great effort to gather his breath again, and Janet came in at the door as he gasped,

"The story was that he—"

"*Story!*" exclaimed Janet, with a scandalized look on her face. "What's this, Robbie? Have you no heart at all that you can let your poor Old Da waste his last breath on stories for you?"

46

"I didn't want him to do that," Robbie protested. "I tried to hush him, but he *would* speak."

"Well, he's quiet now," said Janet, looking down at Old Da; and indeed he was quiet, for the effort of speaking to Robbie had quite exhausted him.

"Away you go, then," Janet went on, "and I'll sit with him until he sleeps."

Robbie nodded; then he leaned down to Old Da and said softly, "Good-night, Old Da."

Old Da looked up at him without making any further attempt to speak, but there was something in his eyes that made Robbie add,

"I'll remember what you said—and I'll do as you told me."

Old Da smiled, just a faint shadow of a smile, but enough to show he had understood; and Robbie went away feeling puzzled by what had happened, yet relieved that Old Da was no longer distressing himself by trying to talk.

That night, however, he found he could not sleep for thinking of what the old man *had* said; and late, very late, when Janet and Elspeth were asleep and even Old Da's breathing had eased, he slipped from his bed and went outside.

It was not dark then, of course, otherwise he would never have gone out like this, for it is in the hours between sunset and sunrise that the trows are free to work their magic. The Shetlands lie so far north, however, that there is no darkness there in summer.

All that happens is a dimming of the light when the sun sets, but the colors stay in the sky for a while. Then the sky becomes white for an hour or two before the next sunrise; and it was into this sort of white night that Robbie ventured.

A quick glance around showed him there were no trows in sight; but just in case there were any lurking invisibly around, he did as Old Da had taught him to do in such situations. He made the sign of the cross on himself, and said aloud,

"God be about me and all that I see."

Immediately then, he knew he was safe, for these are words that trows cannot bear to hear and so they scatter instantly at the sound of them. Without bothering any further about trowie magic, therefore, he climbed the hill above the voe, and sitting down on the grass there he tried to sort out all the questions that had kept running through his mind.

Had Old Da really been trying to tell him something? Something important? Had he really been trying to give warning of some danger that threatened Elspeth? Or had he simply been raving in the grip of his fever?

Robbie stared down to the silky-gray of the voe's waters, noticing the occasional seal which surfaced there; and vague memories of the stories Old Da used to tell him went chasing through his head. *. . . a crystal palace under the sea . . .* Could there be such a thing? *There was another stranger like Finn Learson.* What stranger? And what had this other man to do with the crystal palace of the Great Selkie?

Robbie got tired at last of asking himself such questions, for he could not arrange any answers to them in a way that made sense. Besides which, he told himself, it was time he was going home again. There was a wash of pale gold across the white of the north-eastern sky, and a rim of brighter gold on the horizon as the sun touched it again.

Dreamily, almost on the point of sleep at last, Robbie sat watching this rim of gold grow wider and brighter, and then was suddenly jerked wide awake again by the sight of his father's sixareen coming into the voe.

There was no doubt, either, that it *was* his father's sixareen, for the sun was gilding the heads of the rowers and he could see it gleaming red off Nicol Anderson's red hair. Another moment or two and he could also see a head of hair that was the same sandy-gold color as Elspeth's and his own—his father's head, rising into the light then dropping back into shadow when he bent to the oar.

With a leap of excitement at his heart, Robbie gathered himself to rise and run down to the shore. But even as he stirred, a sound broke the white-and-gold silence of the morning—the sound of Tam howling at the door of the Hendersons' house. And without being able to tell how or why this should be so, Robbie knew in that instant that his Old Da was dead.

On and on the howls went; and supposing his own life had hung on it, Robbie could not have moved then. As still as if he had been part of the hillside itself, he sat watching the boat coming to rest and all the men climbing out of it. His father was first out, jumping clear even before the boat's prow touched the shingle, and racing up the slope to the house. The other men stayed to beach the boat, then they too hurried up the slope.

All except one, Robbie saw; the big, dark-haired one who was Finn Learson.

But that, he argued, feeling his mind beginning to come alive again—that was only natural. Finn Learson was no kin or neighbor to Old Da. He was a stranger, an incomer to Black Ness; and it was not proper for a stranger to thrust himself into a house of mourning.

Yet still the dark figure by the boat seemed somehow threatening to Robbie, and Old Da's words rang in his mind—*"Don't trust him, Robbie. Don't trust him."* Then Finn Learson lifted his head and looked up the hill to where Robbie sat. He moved, and very leisurely began to climb the hill towards him.

Now, Robbie told himself, now was the time for *him* to move—to run down the hill towards the house, to his father and mother and Elspeth, to his friend Nicol, and all the other men, to the people he knew and trusted. And then he asked himself why, *why* should he run? What did he have to fear from Finn Learson?

There was no answer to this question. There was nothing except a big man coming towards him, dark and tall against the sun—and fear in his heart; a fear he could not understand or explain.

Finn Learson was almost up on him now, and still he sat where he was. Then Finn Learson was standing looking down at him, and saying in his deep, pleasant voice,

"The news is bad, it seems."

"Aye," Robbie answered flatly. "Old Da is dead."

"That's bad—that *is* bad," said Finn Learson, sighing and shaking his head.

Robbie stared up at him, trying to make out the expression on his face, but the sun was still behind Finn Learson, and it was only a patch of shadow that met Robbie's eye.

There was a long silence, then Finn Learson spoke again, still very mildly and pleasantly.

"Were you much with him before he died, Robbie?"

Why? Robbie wondered to himself. *Why did Finn Learson want to know that?* "Old Da liked my company," he said aloud. "I sat with him a lot."

"I know, I know. You were his favorite." Finn Learson said this so soothingly that Robbie felt sudden tears pricking his eyelids. For a moment, indeed, he almost forgot to feel wary. Then Finn Learson dropped to one knee beside him, and for the first time, Robbie saw his face.

"And he told you things, didn't he, Robbie?" the face said.

Its voice was still quiet and soothing. The face itself was young and handsome. Yet still Robbie shrank back from it, for the eyes—the gleaming dark eyes in the face were hard as stone; and he was mortally afraid of them.

"What did he tell you, Robbie?" the face persisted. And with Old Da's *"Don't trust him. Don't trust him"* ringing now like a peal of bells in his head, Robbie gathered every ounce of courage he possessed, and answered firmly,

"Nothing! My Old Da told me *nothing*!"

7

Funeral Magic

It was two days later that the funeral of Old Da Henderson took place, and he was a man who had been so popular that this was a great occasion.

All the men of Black Ness came home from the *haaf* that day. There was a tremendous gathering of other mourners as well, and in spite of their own grief for Old Da, the Hendersons were pleased by such respect. They were also determined to carry out all the old funeral customs of the island the way Old Da would have wanted them to do; and so, just before they were all about to start for the burying-ground, Peter came out of the house carrying the straw from the mattress of Old Da's bed.

The minister was out there with his Bible under his arm. All the mourners stood silently gathered, with the coffin in their midst. Robbie was waiting with a lit torch in his hand, and when his father had set the straw on the ground, he thrust this torch into the heart of it.

Now this custom of burning the bed straw of a dead man—the *lik* straw, as it was called—was a very ancient custom on the island. It was also very superstitious, for everyone there believed that a footprint could sometimes be seen in the ashes of the *lik* straw; and this footprint would show which member of the dead man's family would be next to die.

Naturally enough, therefore, the minister would have nothing to do with such a custom, which he thought was very un-Christian. He stood well back from the fire to show his disapproval of it; and since Finn Learson was a stranger to the island and its customs, he also took care to stand back from the fire. Everyone else, however, got as close as they could to it, and every eye was fastened intently on the flames.

For a few moments the straw burned fiercely, then the flames sank and dwindled quickly to nothing more than a lick of fire. A thin column of smoke rose from the smoldering ash, drifting and slowly unwinding in the still summer air. But now the mourners were no longer silent, for they could see a bird winging heavily towards this smoke—a black bird, like a crow, but much bigger than any crow.

It was a raven—the bird of ill omen, the bird with the hoarse and arrogant cry that foretells death, and the mourners muttered fearfully to one another at its approach. They muttered again as it pitched down to light on the roof of the Hendersons' house.

And standing by with a face as sour as if he had been sucking a lemon, the minister opened his Bible to show how much he disapproved of this further show of superstition.

The Henderson family, however, did not hear the mourners and they did not heed the minister; for now the ash was settling, soft and gray, with the last trace of red gone from it. And there, in the middle of all the little mounds and hollows of its final pattern, was the clearly marked shape of a footprint.

The shape was a small and neat one—the print of a girl's shoe; and staring at it like someone in a dream, Elspeth recognized it for her own. Slowly she lifted one foot and advanced it towards the ashes. Carefully she set the foot down again, and the sole of her shoe fitted perfectly into the shape of the print.

Janet went sheet-white at this, for it was not in the natural order of things, of course, that anyone so young as Elspeth should be the next in the family to die. Peter and Nicol Anderson were also much shaken by this turn of events, and each of them put out a hand to draw Elspeth hastily back from the ash.

"It can't be!" said Janet then, staring in dismay at Peter as she spoke. "Elspeth's so much younger than either of us—it can't be her turn next!"

This was altogether too much for Elspeth, who gave a little cry and slid in a dead faint to the ground.

"Now look what you've done," said Nicol in dismay; and Janet shouted,

"Then help me to undo it, will you, instead of just standing there like a great, stupid gowk!"

As usual with men in such situations, however, Nicol had no ideas at all in his head. Peter was equally useless, and seizing hold of Robbie, Janet commanded,

"Off to the house with you, and get some water!" Then, shoving Robbie away from her, she got down on her knees beside Elspeth.

Robbie's mind was all in a daze over what had happened; but he took off instantly, all the same, and was back in less than a minute with a jug of water in his hand. The situation had changed, however, even in that short time, for now it was Nicol who knelt beside Elspeth. Elspeth herself had come round from her faint, and Nicol was raising her from the ground. Finn Learson had stepped forward to help him with this, and the minister was stalking back and forth, raging at everyone.

"No one with any sense would believe such superstitious nonsense!" he shouted, and Nicol said awkwardly,

"Of course, minister, of course. And Elspeth will be fine now."

Elspeth, however, was still far from fine, and she could see very well the doubt and fear on all the faces around her. Piteously she glanced around for further comfort, and realized that Finn Learson was smiling at her.

"Do *you* think the minister is right?" she asked him, and cheerfully he told her,

"I'll tell you what I think! You will live to wed the man of your choice, and you will be rich when you wed. And what is more, you will be beautiful to the end of your days!"

"Thank heaven for one man with common sense!" the minister exclaimed; but it flashed across Robbie's mind then that Elspeth would not be rich if she married Nicol Anderson.

Nicol had the same thought, it seemed, for he flushed to the roots of his red hair as Finn Learson spoke, and tried to draw Elspeth back towards himself. Elspeth had listened eagerly to Finn Learson's words however; and now, with a flush of hope on her face, she brushed Nicol's hand away.

"Is that truly how it will be?" she asked Finn Learson. "Are you sure of that?"

Finn Learson fixed her gaze with his own bright, dark-brown one. "As sure as anyone can be of anything," he told her; and the minister echoed,

"Of course he's sure! And now, for goodness sake, lassie, let him take you back to the house to have a rest while we get on with the real business of the day!"

"I'll take her," said Nicol, looking annoyed at this.

"You will not!" the minister told him, glaring.

"He is not a member of my parish, but you are. And so you will stay here with the rest to listen to what I have to say now!"

Nicol scowled at this, but dared not disobey; and while Finn Learson took Elspeth off, talking soothingly to her all the while, the minister gave everyone a fierce lecture on the folly of letting superstition rule their lives.

So the whole business of the *lik* straw came to an end, with everyone feeling so shamed by the panic it had caused that they were only too anxious to put it all behind them. Besides which, there was something else happened that day which very quickly took the thoughts of the Henderson family in quite another direction.

It was an hour or so after the funeral that this second event took place. The minister had gone stalking off with his Bible under his arm and a face as sour as ever. The mourners had all scattered to their own homes. The sixareens of the men who had come home from the *haaf* for the funeral had sailed away out of the voe, and the only boat left drawn up on the shingle was Peter's sixareen.

It was to make sure Elspeth had recovered from her fright that Peter had lingered. But, as it happened, he need not have bothered about this. Elspeth was so much herself when the others got back to the house that she had made tea for everyone; and so now Peter and his crew were sitting around in the but end, having a last cup of this tea and a last talk about Old Da before they also took their departure.

Finn Learson was there too, of course, but he sat in a far corner keeping himself to himself as usual. Robbie was another who took no part in this last talk, since he had gone to the window to watch the seals in the voe while he thought his own thoughts about Old Da.

It was still Robbie, however, who brought the conversation to an end, for his view from the window showed him a boat coming swiftly into the voe; and as this boat came closer to the shore, he realized something that sent a great thrill of alarm through him. Quickly he swung round from the window and shouted above the sound of all the other voices in the room,

"Da, listen! There's a boat coming into the voe, and I think it's the Press Gang that's in it!"

Now this was bad news—very bad news indeed, for the Press Gang was the crew that captured men for forced service in the Navy; and this was a fate to be dreaded in those days when life aboard a naval warship was such a hard and brutal affair. Moreover, with all the men of the islands being naturally good seamen, the Press Gang was especially active there. And so, to every man in the room then, Robbie's shout was a warning of desperate and immediate danger.

8

Finn's Magic

A moment of deathly silence followed Robbie's warning, then Peter headed a mad rush for the window.

"It *is* the Press Gang," said he, staring in dismay at the boat in the voe. "And we're trapped here, because their boat is between us and the open sea. We can't escape to the hills, either, because they'll sight us the instant we're out the door—and already they have the house within range of their pistols!"

"Then we'll just have to risk being shot," Nicol declared. "Better to make a run for the hills, Peter, than stay tamely here to be taken."

"No!" Finn Learson spoke suddenly, surprising them all with the first word he had uttered since the funeral. Every face turned towards him, and calmly he went on,

"There's no need to take such a risk, Nicol. Stay here, and—"

"But we're trapped if we stay here," Nicol interrupted angrily. "You heard Peter say that!"

"I did," agreed Finn Learson, calm as ever. "But Peter was wrong, for you can still escape *if you stay here long enough to let me draw them away from the beach*. Make a dash for the sixareen then; head out to sea, and that will be you well clear of danger!"

"But they're certain to capture you, if you do that," Nicol protested. "And that means you'll be the sacrifice for all of us."

Finn Learson moved to the door, smiling his strange and secret little smile as he went. "It doesn't mean anything of the kind," he answered. "Not with the game *I* will play! And don't wait for me once you do have the chance to escape, for I'll easily find my own way back to the fishing station. And that's where I'll meet you all again."

He had the door open with this, and was gone before anyone could say another word. Nicol stared after him, frowning, and then said flatly,

"He's a fool. He'll be one against twenty out there!"

This started another rush for the window, but Peter soon put a stop to that.

"Get back from there!" he shouted. "Can you not see he wants them to think he is the only man in the house, and that it will spoil his plans if they notice *your* faces at the window?"

The crew of the sixareen fell back from the window, casting sheepish looks at one another; and Peter told them,

"That's better. But we still need a lookout to tell us what's happening—and so, on *you* go, Robbie. They'll not think anything of a boy watching them!"

Robbie darted to the window, and saw the Press Gang's boat only a few yards from the shore.

"The boat's coming in fast," he reported. "It's nearly there!"

"And Finn Learson?" Peter demanded. "What's *he* doing?"

"Nothing yet," Robbie answered. "He's just sauntering down to the beach as if he hadn't a thought in his head except to pass the time of day with the Press Gang!"

"Then they'll have him for sure," Peter exclaimed. "There's not a chance he'll escape now."

"That's the way it looks," Robbie agreed. "Their boat's almost touching. . . . It's in! It's grounded on the shingle!"

The men in the boat began leaping ashore, waving and calling to the tall figure sauntering to meet them. Finn Learson called cheerfully in reply; and with broad grins at the thought of someone too stupid or too ignorant to run from them, the men of the Press Gang scrambled forward over the shingle.

Still Finn Learson did not run. The distance between him and the Press Gang narrowed to a few feet, and the officer who led the chase stretched out a hand to seize him.

"They're grabbing him!" Robbie shouted. But even as the words left his lips, Finn Learson leaped back out of the officer's reach. "But they've missed!" Robbie added triumphantly. "And he's running now—running just ahead of them along the beach."

"Get ready to move," Peter warned the rest of the crew, and they all gathered around him at the door of the but end.

Down on the beach the Press Gang continued to chase after Finn Learson, laughing like men playing a game as they ran clumsily over the shingle. And it *was* only like some horrible game to them, Robbie realized, for it still looked as if they would have no trouble in capturing him.

He was keeping ahead of them, but only just ahead; and with every step of the chase it looked as if they *must* seize hold of him. Yet still, every time a hand was about to close on him, he seemed to melt out of its grasp as if he were no more solid than smoke. Then once again, he was magically that little bit ahead; and as Robbie stared in fascination at this, Peter urged,

"Come on, boy. Tell us what's happening now."

"Finn Learson's playing the wounded bird," Robbie answered then, for that was exactly what Finn Learson was like—a bird trailing along with a pretense of a broken wing that would make it an easy capture, and all the time leading its pursuers further and further away from its nest. "But it's the way he's doing it, Da! It's like magic the way he's just not there when they grab at him!"

"Leave imagination out of this, and stick to facts," Peter said grimly. "Are they far enough away from the sixareen yet?"

"No, but they soon will be," Robbie told him, for now Finn Learson had reached the grassy slope that led from the beach to the cliffs rising on one side of the voe, and the pace of the hunt was quickening. The officer in charge of the Press Gang was losing patience with it too, and suddenly it was no longer a game as he spread out his men and began to close them like a net around Finn Learson.

But even this did not succeed, for suddenly also, Finn Learson was escaping from the net with an ease that seemed more than ever magical; for now he was moving so fast that his feet seemed to skim the ground with no effort at all, and he was no longer like a man running. He seemed to be flying, instead; and far from closing in on him, the men of the Press Gang were being left well behind.

The officer in charge of them drew his pistol and pointed it at the flying figure.

"They're shooting at him!" Robbie cried, and instantly Peter ordered the others,

"Run for the boat! And shout as you run, to draw their attention off him!"

The shot from the officer's pistol sounded at that moment, and flinging open the door of the but end, Peter rushed outside. The others piled after him, yelling at the tops of their voices and running as hard as they could for the beach. The men of the Press Gang turned towards the sound of the yells; and crowding to the door to watch from there, Robbie and Janet and Elspeth saw them shaking their fists at the way they had been tricked.

Robbie took his last look at Finn Learson disappearing far into the distance, and then turned his attention to the voe. Half of the sixareen's crew had already got their boat pushed out and were holding it steady. The others were busy setting the Press Gang's boat adrift. The Press Gang, meanwhile, were running back to the beach, firing their pistols as they ran. But Finn Learson had taken them a good bit out of range, and well before they were within real firing distance, the sixareen was pulling strongly out into the voe.

"They'll be well out to sea before the Press Gang can get *their* boat back," Janet decided then. "They're safe now!" And smiling with relief at this, she went back into the house to wash the tea-cups.

Elspeth stayed to watch the Press Gang's rage at finding their boat afloat in the voe. "That Finn Learson," she remarked; "it was some trick he played them!" Then, a little scornfully, she added, "It's a pity Nicol couldn't have been so clever."

"That's not fair," said Robbie, flying immediately to Nicol's defense. "Nicol was brave enough to want to make a break for the hills. And anyway, he couldn't have played the wounded bird—not the way Finn Learson did, for it was like magic the way he kept slipping through their hands. And it was like magic, too, the turn of speed he put on at the end of the chase."

"You'll be in trouble if Mam hears you talking nonsense like that," Elspeth told him sharply. "You know she's forever complaining about the way you let your imagination run away with you."

"And you'll be in trouble too, if you let Nicol hear you say such things about him," Robbie retorted. "He might even think twice about marrying you then!"

"And who said I wanted to marry Nicol?" Elspeth demanded.

Robbie stared at her. "But I thought—" he began, and Elspeth interrupted,

"Oh, yes. Everybody thinks I want to marry Nicol because he wants to marry me. Well, maybe I did at one time. But maybe now I'll marry somebody quite different. Somebody . . ."

"Well?" demanded Robbie, as Elspeth's voice tailed off. "Who's this somebody?"

Elspeth smiled to herself. "Somebody rich," she said teasingly. "What do you think of that, Robbie?"

"I think you're daft," Robbie told her. But lying in

his box bed that night when all the excitement was over, he remembered that it was Finn Learson who had put this idea into her head in the first place. *You will live to wed the man of your choice, and you will be rich when you wed.* That was what he had said to her at Old Da's funeral. And now, thought Robbie, it sounded very much as if he had been encouraging her in this same idea of a rich marriage!

For a while longer he lay thinking about this, and wondering how far Elspeth might have believed anything Finn Learson had told her since the funeral. The uncanny way Finn Learson had avoided the Press Gang came back to his mind. Old Da's warning *Don't trust him* rang in his head, and sleep began to seem very far away.

But maybe Elspeth was wakeful too, he thought; and if she was, he would have a word with her about it. Then he would know for sure if *she* had trusted Finn Learson! Cautiously, quietly, Robbie slid open the door panel of his bed, and looked across the ben room.

The door panel of Elspeth's bed was open. She was sleeping, lying very still with her hands on the cover and her long hair spread out like a fan on the pillow behind her. The white night of summer had crept into the ben room to lie pale across her, making her face ghostly, turning the gold of her hair to silver; and seeing her like this, a strange idea seized hold of Robbie.

The *lik* straw and the raven, he thought, had foretold death for Elspeth; but Finn Learson had said she would live to wed the man of her choice. And now, lying there all white and silver in the white night, she was indeed like a girl dressed for her bridal. But she still did not look like Elspeth asleep. She looked like the ghost of Elspeth—*like Elspeth already dead!*

Shivering, Robbie closed the door panel of his own bed, and was immediately enclosed again in safe, warm dark. Yet still this did not shut out the vision of Elspeth dressed for some deathly bridal. Still it did not banish the uneasy feeling that the vision was linked in some way to his own sense of something uncanny about Finn Learson.

Tossing about and about as he tried once more to sleep, Robbie thought miserably that Old Da would have understood this uneasiness. But Old Da was dead. And so now there was no one who would understand, no one at all he could turn to; for now there was no one except himself who even suspected there was anything uncanny about Finn Learson.

9

Deep Water

It was at harvest time each year that the *haaf* season ended and all the men came home to Black Ness. Finn Learson got a hero's welcome then, of course, and he rose even higher in Peter and Janet's favor when he offered to stay on to help with the harvest on *their* croft. Even when this work was over, however, he still lingered, and the reason for this was soon plain. It was Elspeth who had been the attraction for him all along, it seemed, for now he was beginning to court her with all the charm at his command.

There were various opinions about this situation, of course. Nicol was furious about it, but Elspeth was delighted to have no less than two handsome young men courting her. The rest of the folk in Black Ness saw no harm in it at all—how could they, indeed, when they were all still of the opinion that any strangeness about Finn Learson was due to his being a foreigner?

Only Robbie thought differently, and he was utterly dismayed by the idea that Elspeth might even consider marrying Finn Learson. But supposing she did, he argued to himself, that would make nonsense of the words, *You will be rich when you wed*; for how could Elspeth be rich if she married Finn Learson, any more than she would be if she married Nicol?

The weeks after harvest time slid by with Robbie still uneasily pondering this; and meanwhile, Peter and Janet agreed that they were still glad to see Finn Learson staying on with them. He was a great help on the croft, after all, and he was company for Peter now that Old Da was dead and Nicol had turned so awkward over this courtship business. Moreover—as they were both fond of saying—the favors were far from being all on their side, considering what they owed him over the matter of the Press Gang.

Indeed, it seemed to Robbie, things had now got to the stage where Finn Learson could do no wrong in his parents' eyes; and since the same Robbie had a great respect for his parents, he began at last to wonder if his own thoughts about Finn Learson might perhaps be a bit on the foolish side.

After all, as he had to admit to himself, he had no really good grounds for these thoughts—just his own imagination, in fact, and the last rambling words of a sick old man. Besides which, he was finding Finn Learson a much more talkative man now that Old Da was dead, and quite willing to speak in a friendly way of the roving life he had led.

"Once, on the shores of Greenland," he told Robbie, "a man came at me with a knife to kill me—see, I bear the mark of his knife to this very day, in this long white scar of the healed wound in my shoulder. . . ."

Then on he went, spinning many another tale of strange adventures in far countries. And never once did Robbie dream that all this friendliness might be just a device for drawing him into the same snare of charm that had already begun to hold Elspeth!

There was something else, too, which lulled Robbie's fears at that time and drove other forms of imagining from his mind, for it was in the slack season after harvest each year that he went to school. And that particular year, he had begun to study navigation.

Now this was a subject which could take a Shetland boy far—perhaps even as far as commanding his own whaling ship—and Robbie thought it would be a grand thing to sail north, and ever northwards, in pursuit of the great whale. So it happened that he began to think ever less about Finn Learson; and it was with grand dreams of whaling ships in his head that he set off each day for the schoolhouse on the far side of the hill, to study with the rest of the boys in Black Ness.

This left him with only weekends for the other great interest which always occupied him at that time of the year, and which was therefore another thing that took his mind off Finn Learson; for it was then—

from about the middle of September to the end of October—that all the selkie pups were born.

Robbie knew every place where these were to be found, of course, from all the previous years he had gone with Old Da to visit them. And so, every Saturday he could persuade his father to let him have the boat, he was away by himself to the cliffs rising steeply from the west side of the voe.

This was where the sea had made deep cuts in the rock face—the kind of cut with a name that is sounded "yoe," although it is spelled "geo." This was where the great, dark-gray bull seals came ashore to fight for mastery of the shingle beach at the inner end of each geo. This was where the sleek and shining cow seals came ashore also, to have their pups. And this was where Robbie hoped one day to realize his great longing to pick up one of these pups so that he could learn what a seal felt like.

Not that he would take any risks in that, he assured himself when he remembered Old Da's warnings and felt his conscience pricking him. To begin with, he would choose a small geo where there was only likely to be a small nursery of pups with a few cow seals and probably only one bull seal. Also, he would not go ashore at all if the bull was there to guard the beach, and he would take care to hold the pup so that it could not possibly bite him.

With all this in mind then, Robbie fixed that year on a geo that exactly suited his purpose; and patiently every Saturday he visited it, until at last there came the moment he had planned. Eight white seal pups lay on the tiny beach at the inner end of the geo. There was no sign of the bull seal which usually lay roaring there—no sign even of a single cow seal flopping about on the beach, or sliding gracefully through the water.

With his heart hammering out a great drumbeat on his ribs, Robbie let the boat ground gently on the shingle. Stepping knee-deep into the water, he edged the prow on to the stones. Then, moving as silently and cautiously as possible, he approached the nearest of the pups and knelt beside it.

The pup's fur was thick and wet; but the wetness did not seem to bother it, for it was sound asleep, lying on its back with its flippers in the air. Robbie stared at the sleeping pup. It was the first time he had ever seen one at such close quarters, and he could feel the desire to touch it becoming quite over-powering. Gently he reached out a hand, and laid it on the thick, white fur.

The pup's great, round eyelids snapped open. Its mouth opened also, showing two rows of very white, very sharp teeth. Rolling quickly over on to its belly, it made an angry, hissing noise at Robbie. Then, with strong, rapid movements of its flippers, it began pulling itself away from him. Robbie stared after it, swallowing his disappointment as best he could before he turned to the next pup.

This one was also lying on its back, and it seemed even more sound asleep than the first pup had been, for it hardly stirred at all when Robbie ventured a gentle hand on its fur. Cautiously he knelt beside it. With his right hand supporting himself on the shingle, he let his left hand travel slowly, very slowly, across the pup's soft, wet fur. And slowly, slowly, as Robbie's fingers caressed it, the pup awakened.

It stretched, tail and flippers quivering. It made little contented mewing noises, and its head rolled round to rest against Robbie's right forearm. Its eyes opened; great, dark-brown, shining eyes as round as buttons, that stared soulfully up at him.

Robbie began to tremble with the effort not to laugh at this look. The pup was still leaning its head against his right arm, and when he thought he had control of himself, he slipped his left arm around the other side of its body. Carefully then, he gathered the pup clear of the shingle; and rose, holding it cradled in his arms.

It was astonishingly heavy, he found, for such a young creature. And even more astonishing was the heat that came from its damp little body. Holding it, thought Robbie, was like holding a little furnace against his chest.

The black nails on the underside of the pup's flippers caught his attention, and he put one finger against them to see what it would do. Immediately it bent its flipper so that it could grip the finger with these nails, and there was such strength in the grip that Robbie realized there was no way of breaking it except by laying the pup down. Unwillingly, he did so, and then saw the reason for the power of the pup's grip as it bent its flippers again and used the nails to pull itself rapidly away over the shingle.

The other pups on the beach were all awake, their heads turning towards him, their bright, brown-button eyes staring. Robbie approached them one by one, stepping gently, going down on one knee beside them; but the pups would have none of him. They hissed, showing rows of sharp white teeth as the first pup had done. Even the pup he had lifted was unfriendly, now that it was wide awake and could sense the alarm of the others; and resigning himself to this at last, Robbie walked back to the boat.

But still, he told himself, he had done what he had set out to do. He had discovered at last what a selkie *felt* like, and so he had learned something that even Old Da had never been able to teach him—quite apart from which, it had been fun to hold the pup!

Feeling greatly pleased with himself as he came to this conclusion, Robbie considered what he could do next, and wondered if he should head for one of the big geos where he knew there was a nursery of over fifty pups. He could take the boat into the geo, he thought, and from a safe distance there he could watch the three bull selkies that roared challenges to one another as they guarded the beach. And he could count the pups, to see if any more had been born since his last visit!

This last thought decided him on what he wanted to do, and bending strongly to the oars, he headed for the big geo.

It was not far away. Twenty minutes of rowing like this brought him to the entrance channel, and with careful strokes, he backed the boat through this narrow passage. In the wider water beyond, he turned the boat; then, gently feathering as Old Da had taught him, he sat staring at every detail in the scene around him.

The water lapping the boat was deep and green, the color of melted emeralds. The high cliff walls of the geo were wet black, streaked with dull green veins of serpentine. The upward slope of the shingle beach at the geo's inner end was backed by a great jumble of larger stones; and above this jumble, the empty mouth of a cave yawned, huge and black.

On the beach itself, three bull seals reared up, bellowing at one another. And everywhere around the great, grayish-black forms of the bulls, right from the mouth of the cave down to the edge of the emerald water, was a mass of cow seals and their pups.

The sight of the boat had already sent these cow seals heading for the water; and soon, as Robbie rowed closer inshore, they were gliding all around him. He had other things on his mind at that moment, however, and paying no attention to the graceful forms of the cow seals, he prepared for his count of the pups.

He would have to stand up in the boat to make this count, he decided; otherwise, he would not get a clear view of the pups that lay among the big boulders at the back of the beach. But standing up in the boat need not unbalance it, of course—not if he used the trick he had learned along with all the other boys of Black Ness playing around with boats in the shallows of the voe.

Carefully shipping one of his oars on this decision, Robbie slid the other one over the stern of the boat. Then, rising to his feet and holding this second oar almost upright against the stern, he made quick, gentle little movements that sent the boat sculling steadily along the line of the shore.

The three bull seals roared again, as if in astonishment at this sight. The pups kept up a shrill mewing for their vanished mothers; and, rearing chest-high out of the water, the cow seals themselves began to make the sort of noise that cow seals do make at this particular time of the year.

Robbie quite forgot to count then, for this noise from the cow seals was a high, sweet one that sounded like human voices sliding up a scale and echoing eerily between the steep walls of the geo. Also, it was something he had never heard before, in spite of all the times he had watched seals, and he was quite entranced by it. Maybe, he thought, it was this that Old Da had been thinking about when he told that long-ago story about selkie singing. . . .

Then suddenly at the back of his mind, he found a different sort of memory stirring. He *had* heard this noise before, he realized. It was the singing sound he had heard from his father's fiddle on Finn Learson's first night on the island!

The boat began to rock under him as his mind wandered further down this track, and he sculled fast to try to bring it back to an even keel. It swung in a half-circle, bringing him round to face the cliff at the inner end of the geo; but where the line of the cliff-top had been bare a moment before, there was now a man standing. With a jerk of surprise, Robbie recognized the man as Finn Learson, and it was this startled movement that finally cost him his balance.

The boat rocked wildly, snatching the oar from his grasp, and he pitched overboard. The emerald water closed over him. The boat was spun away by the force of his splashing plunge, and he surfaced with his mouth open on a yell, for the water was very deep and he could not swim so much as a single stroke.

A shout from the clifftop answered his yell, but Robbie was struggling too madly to hear this. Water sang in his ears. Water blurred his vision, so that black cliff and gray sky and emerald water became nothing but colors jumbling in a confused mass around him. Yet still he managed to gulp enough air to keep from choking; for the fact of the matter is that even a person in Robbie's position can stay afloat like this for a good minute before he goes right under.

No one had ever told *him* this, however, and so the terror of drowning was like a frenzy on him. Moreover, he was too blinded by water to see Finn Learson starting down towards him, and leaping swift as a cat from ledge to ledge on the cliff face.

Half-way down the cliff Finn Learson paused, balanced for a blink of an eye on his perch, then dived; and Robbie's first hint of rescue was the splash and surging backwash of this dive. A second later he felt a hand catch hold of his hair. An arm closed round him, pinning his threshing hands to his sides. A voice breathed in his ear,

"Easy, now, easy!"

The arm holding him kept his head clear of the water. Robbie drew a great breath of blessed air, and realized that Finn Learson was swimming strongly with him to the boat still drifting a few yards away.

A hand came out over his head, reaching to grasp the boat's gunwale, and Finn Learson prepared to swing him inboard. The arm holding him shifted position, and he realized something else. There was warmth like a furnace heat in the body pressed against his own, and the hand gripping him had fingertips that probed like steel into his flesh.

A quick heave sent him tumbling over the gunwale, and he landed in the bottom of the boat with a clear, sharp memory of the only other time he had ever been held in such a grip, or felt a body so warm. It was that same afternoon, when he had picked up the young selkie—yet how could that be? How could there be selkie warmth in a man's body, and selkie strength in a man's hands?

Robbie's mind began to race, suddenly remembering his Old Da's tales about selkies that took human shape and the Great Selkie that tempted golden-haired girls into his kingdom under the sea. In a flash then, he had the answer to both his questions, and the reason for everything that had ever puzzled him about Finn Learson.

The "dream" of selkie music that had proved to be something he really *had* heard; the stare that had held Tam captive, the gold, the dancing, the magic escape from the Press Gang, the vision of Elspeth dead in bridal white—and above all, the smile, the secret little smile—he understood now the meaning of all these things. He knew now why Old Da had warned it was Elspeth who was in danger!

Finn Learson's hand appeared over the gunwale of the boat. The fingers that looked human and felt as hard as a selkie's nails, tightened their grip, and a terror as sharp as the terror of drowning shot through Robbie; for there was one thing more he could guess at, now that the meaning of all these other things had become clear.

Finn Learson had not rescued him out of kindness, any more than the saving of the sixareen's crew had sprung from that reason. It was only a cunning desire to stand well with his parents that had prompted both actions—which meant he had only to give the slightest hint of his own thoughts now to find that his life would be worth less than an instant's purchase!

Finn Learson heaved himself inboard. Then, with all the friendliness of recent weeks gone from his voice, he asked,

"And what were you doing in this geo, anyway?"

"Counting selkie pups," Robbie answered shakily. "The same as I used to do every year with Old Da."

Finn Learson gave him a long, suspicious look. "You're sure that was *all* you were doing?" he demanded; and for a moment, Robbie found himself feeling more puzzled than afraid.

"Of course I'm sure," said he. "What other reason could I have for being here?"

Finn Learson did not answer this. He took up the single oar left in the boat, and began paddling with it to reach the other oar adrift in the geo; and as he reached out for it, Robbie decided on the sort of remark he knew would be expected from him at that moment.

"I would have drowned if you had not been here," he said awkwardly, "and I owe you thanks for that."

"You were lucky," Finn Learson told him. "I just happened to notice you heading for this geo and kept you in sight from the clifftop. I had the feeling you might get into trouble here, and that was why I was ready for it when you did."

The drifting oar came within his grasp, and drawing it inboard, he added harshly,

"And so keep out of this geo in future, do you hear? It's high time you learned to leave deep waters to those who *can* swim in them."

That could have been meant as advice, thought Robbie; but said in that harsh voice, it sounded more like a warning—or even a threat! Moreover, why had Finn Learson sounded so suspicious of his presence in the geo in the first place?

Crouched in the bottom of the boat, Robbie watched Finn Learson beginning to row, and the nearer the boat drew towards home, the more clearly he saw that he would have to tell *someone* the truth about him. Yet who was there to tell? Certainly not his own Mam and Da, for they would never believe it was the truth—not now that Finn Learson had put them even deeper in his debt with this latest rescue.

Which meant it would have to be Nicol Anderson, Robbie decided eventually. Nicol had everything to gain by believing the truth, after all, and nothing whatever to lose. It would be worthwhile at least trying to make Nicol believe him!

10

Nicol

For two days after the rescue in the geo, Robbie waited his chance to speak alone with Nicol Anderson.

"I need a word with you, Nicol," said he, the moment he found this chance. "A private word about Finn Learson and Elspeth."

"That's none of your business," Nicol told him sharply. "But if you must talk about it, talk to your Mam and Da. *I* don't want to hear what you have to say."

"But you've got to," Robbie insisted. "My Mam and Da thought the world of him even before he saved me from drowning, and now that's happened, they'll not hear a word against him. I'm sure of that, and so what use is it to try talking to them?"

"Then try holding your tongue for a change," Nicol retorted. "You should think shame, anyway, for even wanting to speak against a man who has just saved your life."

"If he had guessed what I was thinking about him," said Robbie miserably, "he would have tipped me back into the water and left me to drown in good earnest. That's something else I know for sure."

"Robbie Henderson!" Nicol exclaimed. "That's a terrible thing to say about anybody!"

"I know it is," Robbie admitted, "but I've got a good reason for saying it about Finn Learson. It came to me suddenly when he was shoving me back into the boat, and I'm certain I know the truth now."

"The truth about what?" Nicol demanded. "You're talking in riddles, boy."

"Then I'll begin at the beginning," Robbie told him. "Do you remember the night he came ashore, Nicol—the night of the storm that wrecked the *Bergen*?"

"Of course," Nicol nodded. "But what's that got to do with it?"

"Just this," Robbie answered. "He came ashore looking like a survivor of that wreck, and so everybody took it for granted that he was. But *he* never claimed to be a survivor. He never spoke about the *Bergen* as *my* ship. Whenever he mentioned it, he called it 'the' ship."

"And what's that but a slip of the tongue?" Nicol asked. "He's a Norwegian, isn't he? At least, the ship was Norwegian, and you can tell from the way he speaks that he's some sort of foreigner. And anyway, if he didn't come from the ship, where could he have come from?"

"I'll get to that in a minute," said Robbie. "But have you noticed, Nicol, that little smile he sometimes gives—as if he was enjoying some secret sort of joke?"

"Well—now you mention it, I suppose I have," Nicol admitted. "But, Robbie—"

"Wait!" Robbie interrupted. "Let me tell you about his first night in our house, Nicol. We had trouble with Tam barking and growling then; but late that night he stared into Tam's eyes, and the creature was frightened of him. It was after we were all in bed that this happened, but *I* saw it because I was wakened by Finn Learson playing on my Da's fiddle."

"Playing what?" Nicol asked curiously. "And why would he do that?"

"I can't tell you why," Robbie admitted, "but I do know *what* he played. It was selkie music—the kind of singing sound that selkies make in the geos at this time of the year—and it was all so strange that I thought afterwards it must have been a dream. Then, just before I fell overboard a couple of days ago, I heard the selkies making the same music and I knew it hadn't been a dream at all."

Nicol stared at this. Then he glanced around to make sure there was no one else within earshot, but it was down at the voe that this conversation took place and there was no one but himself and Robbie there.

"You're talking very strangely now," he remarked. "And I'm not sure I should let you say any more—"

"Yes you must," Robbie interrupted again. "There's the gold coin he gave us, Nicol. Old Da backed me up when I said it must have come from a sunken treasure ship, and Finn Learson never denied that was the case. He just said it was something he had picked up on his travels."

"And so it would be," Nicol argued. "That's what your Da thought it was, anyway—he told me so himself."

"Aye, but Finn Learson never said when or where he had picked it up," Robbie pointed out, "and I think I know the answer to that now. A selkie could dive deep enough to reach a sunken treasure ship, and when Finn Learson pulled me out of the geo, he *felt* like a selkie."

Nicol stared again, then he smiled and said, "Oh aye, Robbie. And what other clues do you have to the 'truth' about Finn Learson?"

"Things my Old Da told me, just before he died," said Robbie, trying hard not to notice Nicol's smile. "He didn't trust Finn Learson, and he told *me* not to trust him. He said it had all happened before—that there was another man had come ashore like Finn Learson. And he said that Elspeth was the one in danger."

Nicol's smile vanished at these last words. "She's in danger of marrying him, if that's what you mean," said he sourly. "I don't need *you* to tell me that."

"But that *is* the danger!" Robbie cried. "I know it is, from—well, from other things my Old Da told me."

"What do you mean by 'other things'?" Nicol demanded. "What sort of things?"

"Well," said Robbie carefully, "it was when I was only a wee boy and he told me about the Great Selkie that rules in the deepest ocean. He has a palace of crystal there, Old Da said, and this palace is roofed with the hair of girls he has tempted into his kingdom and drowned there when they wanted to go back to their own kind—girls with golden hair, like Elspeth's."

Nicol heaved a great sigh of impatience at this point. "But that's only a story," he pointed out. "I heard it myself when I was a wee boy, but even then I didn't believe it was true."

"Neither did I at the time," Robbie admitted. "At least, I wasn't sure about it. But there was something else Old Da told me. He said that selkies love to dance—and you know how true that is of Finn Learson! Moreover, they come ashore to dance, Old Da said; and when that happens, they cast off their skins and take the shape of men. Then he sang to me about the Great Selkie—a bit of an old song that said, *'I am a man upon the land, a selkie in the sea . . .'* And that's what Finn Learson is, Nicol.

That's why Old Da warned me against him—because he had guessed that *Finn Learson is the Great Selkie!*"

"Oh, rubbish!" shouted Nicol, his patience breaking at last, and Robbie backed away in dismay at the anger in his voice.

"But I told you," he protested. "Finn Learson *felt* like a selkie. I know, because I picked up a young selkie that same day, and held it close. And there's another thing, Nicol. The omens on the day of Old Da's funeral—the footprint and the raven. *They* said Elspeth would die, but Finn Learson told her, '*You will live to wed the man of your choice, and you will be rich when you wed.*' That didn't make sense at the time—"

"It still doesn't," Nicol interrupted, but Robbie cried, "It does, it does! Finn Learson is rich—he must be, if he is the Great Selkie, for he can get gold any time he wants. But if Elspeth agrees to wed him, he will carry her off to his kingdom under the sea. And then, to us at least, she *will* be dead!"

Nicol said nothing for a few moments. He just looked at Robbie as if he were really seeing him for the first time and didn't quite know what to make of him. Robbie took his silence for an encouraging sign, however, and so he added,

"There's just one last thing, Nicol. Selkies are the sea-wanderers of the world—you know that! And just think of all the traveling Finn Learson has done. Think of the way he took the chance of going to the

88

haaf, so that he could be out there in the deep water again. Doesn't that help to prove I'm right?"

Nicol shook his head. "I could point you a dozen men on this island as far traveled as Finn Learson," he remarked; and in desperation then, Robbie cried,

"But you've got to believe me, all the same, Nicol. You've got to see how everything fits—the way Finn Learson fooled us all into taking it for granted he had come from the wreck, the gold, the dancing, the selkie warmth I felt from him, the way he is courting Elspeth now—they all add up to the same thing. He's not a man at all—that's the trick he's played on us, and that's the secret behind his smile. He's the Great Selkie come ashore in the shape of a man!"

"If you believe that," Nicol declared, "you'll believe *anything*! That's my opinion, Robbie; my honest opinion. And it's my opinion, too, that it's high time you stopped making up such fanciful tales."

"And what about the selkie music I heard in the geo?" Robbie asked. "I didn't make that up, and it *was* the music Finn Learson played on his first night here. Then there's the dancing and the magical way he seemed to get Tam into his power. I didn't make them up either."

"Och, be reasonable," Nicol protested. "You said yourself you had dreamt the bit about Finn Learson playing the selkie music and getting some sort of hold over Tam."

"But I didn't dream it after all!" Robbie exclaimed. "I said that too, Nicol, and that's the whole point. Besides, the power he put out on Tam wasn't his only piece of magic. It was magic he used too, to save everyone from the Press Gang. I know, because I saw it; and there was no ordinary man could have drawn them on the way he did."

"Oh, wasn't there?" Nicol snapped. "And how do you know what any of us could have done if we'd been given the chance?"

With great dismay then, Robbie saw how he had blundered, and quickly tried to get free of his own trap.

"I didn't mean to insult *you*, Nicol," he began, but Nicol was too annoyed now to let him continue.

"I told you at the beginning that this was none of your business," he said curtly, "and I should have had the sense to stick to that, instead of standing here listening to all this nonsense about the Great Selkie. And now I'll tell *you* one last thing, Robbie. It's a case of 'may the best man win' between Finn Learson and myself, and I'll have the whole island laughing at me if I let a boy of your age bring such nonsense into it. And so don't you dare to say a word to Elspeth of all this, or I'll give you a hiding that will make you wish you had never been born!"

He meant that too, thought Robbie, looking up at Nicol's flushed and furious face; and was all the more impressed by it because Nicol was usually so easy-going, and so friendly with him.

"All right, I won't tell her," he promised, but he looked so forlorn as he said this, that Nicol relented a bit.

"Och, come on," said he. "I've been a bit rough with you, I know; but it's for your own good, Robbie. And later on, maybe, you'll thank me for not letting you make a fool of yourself, as well as of me!"

Robbie looked him straight in the eye. "I'm not the fool around here," he retorted; and turned away, feeling miserable enough at the way things had turned out, but still determined not to let it be the end of the matter.

11

Elspeth

All the rest of that day Robbie tried to think of a
way to get round the promise Nicol had forced out
of him, but by the time evening came he was no
nearer an answer to this problem. Then he and
Elspeth were sent off together to bring the cows in
from the hill; and, for all he knew he would have to
be very cautious about it, he could not help putting
a question or two to her.

"There's something I want to ask you," he began
these questions. "I want to know if you've made up
your mind yet which one you will marry—Nicol,
or Finn Learson."

"I'm not going to tell *you* that," said Elspeth,
looking annoyed. "It's none of your business!"

"Yes, it is," Robbie insisted. "I know a lot of
things that make it my business."

"Do you indeed?" Elspeth teased. "Well, I know
things, too—things Finn Learson himself has told
me."

This was something that made Robbie stop dead in his tracks. "What sort of things?" he asked fearfully. And smiling at the tone of his voice, Elspeth answered,

"Well, to start with, he is not just the common sailorman he seems to be. He travels just for the adventure of it, and he is a great man in his own country."

"And when did he tell you that?" asked Robbie. "Was it on the day of Old Da's funeral?"

Elspeth shook her head, refusing to answer this, but Robbie persisted, "And I suppose that was when he started asking you to marry him?"

"Yes, it was," Elspeth admitted then. "But how did you guess that?"

"Because it makes sense of what he said to you that day," Robbie told her. "If *he* is rich, and you married him, then you would be rich too."

"Yes, I would," said Elspeth defiantly. "And why shouldn't I marry a rich man if I want to?"

Robbie thought of the Elspeth he had glimpsed, lying all white and silver like a girl dressed for her bridal, and yet looking like Elspeth already dead.

"But have you said yet that you will marry him?" he pressed. "Have you, Elspeth?"

Elspeth began to smile. "I told him I would think about it," said she, "and I am still thinking."

"And what about Nicol?" Robbie demanded. "What chance has he with you?"

Elspeth stopped smiling then. She looked instead as

if she would cry at any moment, and at last she said miserably,

"I don't know. I used to think I loved Nicol, and now I just don't know what I feel about him."

"Do you love Finn Learson?" asked Robbie, trembling for fear of what he might hear next, but Elspeth shied away from this question.

"He's very handsome," said she. "He has manners like a prince. He has great charm too, and he says that he loves me."

"That's no answer," Robbie told her. "Do you love him?"

The tears started in good earnest to Elspeth's eyes. "I don't know that either," she confessed. "It was all just a good game at first, pretending not to know which one I preferred. But every time Finn Learson looks at me now, I feel weak. I can't look away from him, and then I *want* to marry him. But I still don't know whether that's because I love him."

"It's because he has managed to get some sort of hold over you," Robbie retorted. "Just like he managed to get a hold over Tam, the first night he was here."

"What nonsense are you talking now?" Elspeth demanded. "Tam has nothing to do with all this! And anyway, I have to think of the future, haven't I?"

With temper beginning to spark through her tears, she started to drive the cows again. "If I

94

marry Nicol," she said, "I'll drive cows every night of my life." Then, with the stick in her hand pointing down the hill to their own house, she added,

"And that will be the kind of house I'll have—a but-and-ben with a thatched roof! But if I marry Finn Learson, I'll be a lady with servants, and live in a great house like a palace, with walls of crystal and a golden roof—"

"You great fool!" interrupted Robbie, bawling at her, for this was more than he could stand now. "That's the Great Selkie's palace you're talking about. *And* it has a golden roof, all right—as you'll prove to your cost!"

Too late then, he remembered the promise he had given Nicol; and while Elspeth stared in astonishment at this outburst, he took to his heels and left her to bring the cows home by herself. Not a word would he say to her afterwards, either, when she questioned him on what it had all meant, and he spent the next few days hoping she would not ask Nicol about it.

Fortunately for him, however, Elspeth was too proud to ask Nicol anything about Finn Learson; and as for Nicol himself, the way he was behaving now certainly did not invite anyone to talk to him. He glowered and gloomed about the place to such an extent, in fact, that everyone began to remark on the change in him, and after a few days of this, he came straight out with what was in his mind.

"I'm not going to be kept dangling like this all winter," he told Elspeth in front of the whole family. "If you won't marry me, I'm going off to ship aboard an ocean-going vessel; and once that's done, you'll never see me again. And so, what do you say? Is it to be me, or it is to be Finn Learson?"

Every eye turned to Elspeth. Robbie waited on tenterhooks for her answer. Nicol stared at her, looking grim and unusually pale. Finn Learson sat without any expression at all on his face. Peter and Janet were simply embarrassed, for they were very fond of Nicol and knew he would make a good son-in-law. On the other hand, Finn Learson had won so much of their favor that they could not help feeling it would be a happy arrangement to have *him* for a son-in-law. Besides which, of course, they still felt very much in his debt over one thing and another.

For a long minute, nobody spoke, and then Janet said quietly, "Nicol's right, Elspeth. It's not right to keep him dangling while you make up your mind."

"At least tell them *when* you'll decide," Peter urged. "Put some sort of date to it, so that we'll all know where we are."

Elspeth had flushed when Nicol spoke, then she had gone pale; but when Peter said this, her color came back to normal.

"Very well," said she, "that's what I'll do. I'll set a date to my decision, and I'll marry the man I choose on that date."

"Make it soon," Nicol said grimly; and looking much more sure of herself now, Elspeth named the date she had in mind. Finn Learson was puzzled by this, however, for the date she had chosen is called *Up Helly Aa* in Shetland, which was a name he could not be expected to understand.

"What's the meaning of that?" he asked suspiciously, and Peter explained,

"It's the last of the twenty-four days' holiday we keep at Christmas—or Yule, as it's called with us—and Up Helly Aa is the festival that ends these holidays."

"It's a good day to choose, too," added Janet, looking anxious to keep the peace, "for we'll all be celebrating then, anyway, and everyone will be in the mood to drink a health to the lucky man."

"Well?" Elspeth asked, looking at Nicol. "Do you agree to that?"

"I haven't much choice," said he ungraciously, at which Elspeth frowned, and turned to ask Finn Learson the same question.

"I agree," he answered her, and Robbie's heart sank to see how he smiled as he spoke, and held Elspeth's gaze with his own.

Instead of making Robbie give up hope, however, this situation made him even more determined to find some way of defeating Finn Learson. There had to be something he could try, he kept telling himself. There had to be someone who would believe what *he* believed; and gradually, out of all this, an idea came to him.

Every morning after that as he walked to school, Robbie carried this idea with him, for the person he had in mind to help him with it was the schoolmaster of Black Ness. Every day, however, he still came home with nothing done about his idea—although no one could really blame him for this—for, to say the least of it, this schoolmaster was an unusual sort of person.

To begin with, he had the nickname of Yarl Corbie, for that is the nickname the raven has in Shetland, and he looked like nothing so much as a huge raven.

His nose was big and beaky. His skin was swarthy. His eyes glittered in a sharp and knowing way. He was tall, but very thin and stooped, and he dressed always in black. Besides which, he always wore a tattered, black, schoolmaster's gown that flapped from his shoulders like a raven's wings. And like the raven, he was solitary in his habits.

There was yet another reason, however, for his nickname of Yarl Corbie. Long ago, it was said, in the days when this schoolmaster was still only an unchristened child, he had been fed on broth made from the bodies of two ravens. This, it was also said, had gifted him with all the powers of a wizard; and it was this, of course, which had given Robbie his idea.

Yet here was the snag to it all. Robbie was deadly afraid of Yarl Corbie; for Robbie, it has to be remembered, was twelve years old at that time, which was certainly not old enough for him to have lost his fear of wizards. It has to be remembered too, that Robbie was Shetland born and bred; which meant that deep, deep down in his blood and in his bones there lived the Shetlander's ancient fear of the raven and its croaking cry of death. Also, it was still dark during the time of his walk to school on these winter mornings, and trows have power in the dark; with the result that his imagination had plenty to work on before he even set foot in the schoolroom.

Day after day, therefore, the same thing happened to him. He set out for school carrying the peat every scholar was supposed to bring each day for the schoolroom fire. In his pocket was the stub of candle he needed to light his lessons, and in his mind floated the splendid idea of calling on Yarl Corbie's wizard powers to help him. Yet still, by the time he reached school each day, all the splendor of his idea had fled; for, by this time also, his fear of the trow-haunted dark had convinced him he would never be able to conquer his equal fear of Yarl Corbie.

As soon as he entered the classroom, he was even more sure of this; for there, as usual, sat Yarl Corbie hunched at his desk with his gown drooping like black wings from his bony shoulders. There was his dark and beaky face, seeming all bones and hollows in the candlelight. There was the glittering eye with its knowing stare. And there as usual in his own heart, was the choking dread that he knew would keep him dumb until the day was over and it was too late to ask what he had meant to ask of Yarl Corbie.

So the days before Christmas raced past for Robbie; and each day, it seemed to him, was a wasted one. Then, a week before Christmas, came the start of the twenty-four days' holiday time. Yarl Corbie announced the break-up of school, and Robbie knew he would *have* to speak that day, or lose his last chance of saving Elspeth.

The determined streak in him suddenly got the upper hand of his fear, and while all the other boys raced outside yelling for joy of the holidays, he moved slowly towards the schoolmaster's desk.

12

Yarl Corbie

The sharp and knowing eye of Yarl Corbie came to rest on Robbie, and nervously he said,

"It's about Finn Learson, the stranger that came ashore the night the *Bergen* was wrecked. I know something about him—something that makes him a danger to my folks."

"Indeed?" Yarl Corbie remarked. "And why mention this to me?"

"Because nobody else will believe me," said Robbie, holding hard to his courage. "But you might—and then you might help me."

Yarl Corbie stared so hard at this that Robbie flushed scarlet. "What kind of help would you want from me?" he enquired.

"The kind that—that folks say you can give," Robbie stammered, then wished the words unspoken again because Yarl Corbie had smiled to hear them, and his smile was not a pleasant one.

Be careful, it warned, and there was warning too in Yarl Corbie's voice as he said,

"We will talk of that once you have said what you have to say."

Robbie took a deep breath. The worst Yarl Corbie could do would be to laugh at his story, he reminded himself. Then quickly, before he could change his mind on this, he blurted out,

"Finn Learson is the Great Selkie."

Not a flicker of surprise crossed Yarl Corbie's face. "I know that," he said so calmly that Robbie could hardly grasp he had heard aright.

"So you believe me?" he asked stupidly, and Yarl Corbie gave a patient sigh.

"Of course," he answered. "It happens that I know a lot more about the Great Selkie than you do. But I should still like to hear how you guessed about him."

Robbie felt his heart give a great bound of excitement. "I noticed things about him," he began, and raced straight on with the rest of his story.

Yarl Corbie listened in dead silence, his beaky face intent, his sharp eyes never leaving Robbie's face. He sat quite still too, and even after Robbie had finished speaking, it was only his eyes that shifted position. The sight of him like this began to make Robbie feel even more nervous than he had been at first, and finally he could stand it no longer.

"How did *you* know that Finn Learson is the Great Selkie?" he dared to ask.

The sharp and knowing gaze flashed back to himself. "Because he told me," Yarl Corbie answered. "He told everyone when he gave his name as Finn Learson—although I was the only one with the wit to see that!"

"I still don't see it," Robbie confessed; and grimly, Yarl Corbie told him,

"You will in a moment. Say his name aloud—say it slowly."

Robbie hesitated, feeling even more puzzled by this command. Then obediently he recited the name, Finn Learson, dragging out the sound as if each part of it was a separate word.

"Exactly!" Yarl Corbie exclaimed. "*Finn, Lear's son*—that is the proper sound of the name, for the Great Selkie is the son of the sea-god, Lear. As for 'Finn,' that is simply an old word for 'magician.' And so there you have the full measure of the bold way that name told everyone exactly who he is—the Magician, who is also Lear's son, the Great Selkie."

Robbie felt a chill in the very marrow of his bones. '*The Magician . . .*' he thought, and once again in his mind's eye, he saw Finn Learson melting like a shadow from the Press Gang's hands, skimming the ground like a creature flying. Then further back still his mind went, to the "dream" of Finn Learson staring Tam into frightened silence.

Tam had sensed the truth from the very beginning, he told himself then, and *that* was why Finn

Learson had needed to get the creature into his power. If only, if only they had all paid more attention to Tam's warning growls that night!

But maybe it was not yet too late. . . . With hope beginning to warm him a little, Robbie waited impatiently for Yarl Corbie to speak again, but the schoolmaster was also thinking his own thoughts and his mind seemed to have drifted far from the present moment.

He had picked up a knife from his desk, Robbie noticed; a long knife with a thin, sharp blade that glittered in the candlelight. With his fingers stroking this blade, he sat for a while longer staring at nothing in particular, but at last he did look at Robbie again.

"It has happened before," he said then, and this was so exactly an echo of Old Da's dying words, that Robbie felt himself gasping.

"There was another time when a stranger came ashore to this island, and the story was that he persuaded a girl to marry him. But he was not a man at all, of course, And he was not young, as he seemed to be. He was the old one, the cunning one, the Magician who is also the Great Selkie. And so, of course, he had a different name that time. 'Aeigirson,' he called himself then, 'Aeigir' being another name for the god of the sea; and the girl who married this stranger, Aeigirson, was never seen alive again."

Yarl Corbie's gaze went back to the knife. His fingers returned to stroking the shining blade. Almost as if talking to himself, he said,

"The girl was young—a bonny girl with golden hair. Her name was Anne."

There was a silence. The blade glittered. Yarl Corbie's fingers moved steadily back and forth along its length.

"Is that the end of the story?" Robbie ventured at last.

Yarl Corbie looked up. "Not quite," he answered. "There was a young man of the islands this girl would have married, and after she was stolen away, he shipped aboard a whaler—to earn money, he said, but his real purpose was to search for the Great Selkie and to kill him. The whaler sailed north; and there, on the coast of Greenland, the man found the Great Selkie in his natural form of a great bull seal. The man drew a knife, and struck out with a blow that was meant to kill; and although he did not succeed in this, he managed at least to give the Great Selkie a sorely wounded shoulder."

Once on the shores of Greenland, I was hunted by a man who came at me with a knife to kill me—see, I carry the mark of his knife to this very day, in this long, white scar of the healed wound in my shoulder. . . .

The echo of Finn Learson's voice sounded in Robbie's mind, and once again he saw Finn Learson turning a smooth brown shoulder to show the mark of a long knife-wound.

"How do you know all about this?" he asked curiously, and was astonished to see Yarl Corbie rise to his feet, his face suddenly all twisted with rage. The hand holding the knife went up as if to strike, and Robbie shrank back in alarm, but the blow was not intended for him.

"Because this is the knife that made the wound," Yarl Corbie said harshly. The upraised arm brought the knife hard down towards the desk, and as the point stabbed into the wood, he added, "And I am the man who struck the blow!"

Robbie stared at the blade quivering in the wood. It was hard to imagine Yarl Corbie as a young man, he thought, and even harder to imagine him as a jealous young man in love with a golden-haired girl. But there was one thing at least he could grasp in all this, and surely that was the very thing that mattered now! Triumphantly, Robbie spoke his thoughts aloud.

"You hated the Great Selkie! You *still* hate him!"

Yarl Corbie leaned forward, glaring. "I know what's in your mind," he snapped. "You think that's reason enough for me to help you now. But you're wrong. I know the things they say of me, here in Black Ness, and I am not going to give them cause to say more."

"But no one would know," Robbie pleaded. "Not

from me, at least. And what's to become of Elspeth if you don't help? She'll be like that other girl—Anne. And that will be your fault."

Yarl Corbie frowned at this, until his eyebrows almost met above his beaky nose. Then he clasped his hands behind his back and began striding up and down, his tattered black gown flapping with every step. He looked more like a big, ungainly raven than ever, thought Robbie, and felt the same old dread seizing him again. There was no way of going back on what he had done, however, and he was impatient now, as well as afraid. Biting his lip, he watched the tall, striding figure, and at last Yarl Corbie said,

"I was young and foolish when I went after the Great Selkie with a knife, but I am old enough and and wise enough now to know that he cannot be killed with any mortal weapon. He cannot be defeated either—not when he has his natural form of a selkie, at least. But there *is* one way of making sure he can do no harm while he has a man's shape; one way only."

Yarl Corbie halted in his stride, and shot one of his knowing looks at Robbie. "I cannot see any hope of your carrying that out," he went on. "But nevertheless, you might as well know something about it —which means that you must first of all discover where he hid his selkie skin when he shed it to come ashore. If you do that, you will have a hold over him that could bend him to your will; for, without that skin, *he cannot return to his kingdom under the sea*."

Robbie stood staring at Yarl Corbie, his heart racing suddenly so fast that he could hardly speak. "But—" he managed, "but I—"

Yarl Corbie held up a hand. "I know," he said. "The search for it would be a hopeless one. There are so many places around the coast of the voe where it could be; so many caves—"

"But I *know* where it is!" interrupted Robbie, shouting. "I know!" And still breathing hard, he rushed on to tell Yarl Corbie about the cave in the geo where he had gone to count the selkie pups.

"So you see," he finished triumphantly, "it *must* be hidden there, or Finn Learson would not have bothered to keep me in sight from the clifftop that day. He only did that because he was afraid I would go into the cave and find the skin. And *that* was what he meant when he said he had a feeling I might get into trouble in the geo!"

A wicked gleam came into Yarl Corbie's eyes, making them sharper and brighter than ever. With one long hand stroking his chin, he murmured,

"You could be right, boy. A cave like that—so handy for reaching Black Ness and yet so well hidden from the houses there—would be a perfect lurking-place for him. He could shed his skin and take human form quite safely there when the time came for him to do so. And from there also, he would find it easy enough to swim ashore as if he had just come from a wreck!"

"Of course," Robbie agreed eagerly. "And the chance came when the *Bergen* was wrecked with all hands drowned, so that there was nobody left to say he was *not* a survivor. Moreover, he knew he would need money of some kind on the island, and the cave would give him somewhere to store his gold, all ready to take ashore with him."

"Yes, yes, that could be the way of it," Yarl Corbie nodded. "Gold from the treasure ships sunk around this island was something he could dive for at any time, but he still needed somewhere to keep it in readiness. And as for the trousers and money-belt he wore that night, they would have been only too easy to acquire, what with so many poor drowned sailor-men floating in the voe then."

Robbie felt a cold shiver at the picture this brought into his mind, but he still pressed on with the rest of what he had to say.

"There's one last thing," he told Yarl Corbie. "When Finn Learson pulled me out of the water that day, he told me, '*It's high time you learned to leave the deep waters to those who* can *swim in them*.' And he warned me to keep out of the geo in future."

"Did he, indeed!" Yarl Corbie exclaimed. "Well, that proves it, boy. The skin *must* be in that cave.

And we had better lay hands on it soon—this very night, in fact—or we may lose the chance it gives for getting a hold over Finn Learson."

"*We*?" Robbie asked uncertainly, and Yarl Corbie looked suddenly taken aback.

"Well . . . " he began, then he walked away from Robbie and stood looking at the knife in the desk. One hand went out to pull it free, and he turned to Robbie again, with the wicked gleam once more lighting his eye.

"Yes, we," he said softly, "because I never thought I would live to be revenged on the Great Selkie, and revenge is very sweet. But mark this, Robbie Henderson. It will take magic to defeat the Great Selkie's magic—and you know what our minister is like! You heard the way he raged against superstition on the day of your Old Da's funeral. And so what do you think he would do if he heard I was indeed practicing the unholy arts that people say I do practice? One word, one hint of that, and he would seize on it to have me banished from the island, or jailed —or maybe something even worse!"

"He'll learn nothing from me," Robbie said earnestly. "Nobody will!"

"That had better be a promise," Yarl Corbie assured him, "or I will be revenged on you also! Now get off home, but be down at the voe at midnight, and we will go together to find that skin."

13

The Skin

Robbie needed no second telling to get off home. He was out the door and away like a shot from a bow, and every step of the way home he was telling himself he would never have the courage to be alone in a boat with Yarl Corbie at midnight. In spite of that, however, he was still powerfully attracted by the thought of finding the Great Selkie's skin, and it was this attraction which finally stiffened his nerve that night.

Long after everyone else was asleep, he was still lying wide-eyed in his box of darkness. His ears were alert for the chimes of the grandfather clock in the but end, and on the first stroke of midnight, he slid open the door panel of his bed. Silently he stepped out on to the cold floor. Silently he bundled into his clothes, and crept barefoot into the but end.

With his shoes still in his hand, he stole past the door that led through to the barn where Finn Learson lay sleeping. Carefully he eased up the latch of the front door, slipped outside, and latched it as carefully behind him.

Above him, the sky was black with the deep, velvety blackness of northern skies in winter. A million stars had burned holes of frosty silver in the velvet black. Frost licked like silver fire over the grass underfoot. Robbie shivered as he bent to put on his shoes; but a frosty night meant there would be little wind, even at sea, and he was glad of that. Running fast and lightly, he headed for the beach, and saw the tall stooped figure of Yarl Corbie waiting for him.

The schoolmaster was standing beside the Hendersons' little boat, and without a word as Robbie arrived beside him, he gave a hand to push it out. The two of them clambered aboard, and Robbie bent to the oars. Yarl Corbie sat opposite him, hunched up into the tail-coat he wore now instead of his black gown, and he spoke only once before they reached the geo.

"Did you tell anyone?"

"No one," Robbie answered, thankful he could speak truthfully.

They reached the narrow entrance passage to the geo—too narrow to allow even a reflection of starlight from the water. Robbie backed the boat in, feeling mortally afraid of what just *might* happen in the darkness of this roofless tunnel; but they came out into the wider water beyond, with Yarl Corbie sitting as silent and motionless as before.

The boat touched the shingle, and he shipped the oars, then leaped ashore. Yarl Corbie came clumsily after him, and they pulled the boat up on to the beach.

"Up there—right at the back of the rocks," whispered Robbie, pointing to where the cave lay; and reaching inside his coat, Yarl Corbie brought out a piece of candle and a tinder-box.

"We'll need these," he remarked, then motioned Robbie on.

Robbie had forgotten it would be quite dark inside the cave, and this reminder was enough to make him determined *he* would not be the first to enter it. He clambered on over the rocks, hearing Yarl Corbie following close behind, and at the mouth of the cave he turned to say nervously,

"We'd better light the candle now."

A sound that might have been a chuckle came from Yarl Corbie. "Afraid of the dark, are you?" he jeered, and the next instant Robbie felt a large hand grasping him by the scruff of the neck and forcing him forward into the cave.

Darkness stole his eyesight, smothered him, ate him up. He cried out, gaspingly, then tore himself free of Yarl Corbie's grip and backed until he hit the wall of the cave. A laugh echoed hollow in his ears. The laugh was followed by the sound of Yarl Corbie striking the flint of his tinder-box.

A spark leaped golden through the darkness. The little red flare of the tinder came next. Then at last, as Yarl Corbie lit the candle from the flare, there was a small, but growing pool of real light. The beaky dark face of Yarl Corbie loomed into the light, his eyes searching out the cowering figure of Robbie.

"You did that just to frighten me!" Robbie accused him shakily, and Yarl Corbie smiled the smile that was not pleasant to see.

"That's right," he answered. "There's nothing like a taste of fear to remind you of what could happen if you break the promise you made me!"

The light flickered for a moment as he raised the candle high. He waited till the flame steadied, then turning slowly about, he let its light spread through the cave.

The sealskin was there, lying spread right out to cover a wide rock shelf a few feet from the floor of the cave. The fur of it was the color of Finn Learson's hair—dark, almost black, streaked with silvery gray—and it shone so richly that it seemed to turn the whole pool of candlelight into gleaming black and glittering silver.

Yarl Corbie and Robbie stood staring at it, both of them struck quite dumb at the sight. The empty sockets of the head on the selkie skin stared back at them, and after a few moments of this, Robbie found he could no longer face the eeriness of that empty stare. He turned his head away, and the movement broke the spell of silence in the cave.

"Well, there it is," Yarl Corbie said triumphantly.

"The Great Selkie's skin! And we two are the only two in the world who have ever seen it like this!"

Robbie nodded, and asked nervously, "And what do we do now?"

"You take this," said Yarl Corbie, handing him the candle. Then, much to Robbie's horror, he reached up and pulled the skin down from the shelf as casually as he would have pulled a blanket off a bed. "And I take this!" he added, as the skin came tumbling off the shelf.

Bundling the great pile of it into his arms, he was about to turn away from the shelf, but Robbie's eye had caught a sudden glimpse of something else there.

"Look!" he exclaimed, pointing to the back of the shelf, and Yarl Corbie looked where he pointed.

There was a gleam of gold there, a gleam from a scatter of golden coins that had lain hidden under the skin.

"Fetch one down and let me have a look at it," Yarl Corbie commanded.

Gingerly Robbie stretched a hand out to one of the coins, and one glance as he passed it to Yarl Corbie was enough to tell him it was the same as the gold coin winking on the mantelpiece at home.

"So you were right all along the line," Yarl Corbie remarked, turning the coin curiously over between his fingers. "And to think how bold he was all along the line too, with all the hints he gave you of the truth behind it!"

*. . . something I picked up on my travels . . . take
the gold, for it may still cost more than you think to
have me here . . . a keepsake of me when I have gone
back to my own country . . . remember it did not
seem half so bright to me as the gold of your daughter's hair . . .*

The hints Yarl Corbie had mentioned raced
through Robbie's mind again, and he wondered how
long it had taken Old Da to make sense of these. Not
long, he realized, remembering the long, hard look
Old Da had given on the day he asked Finn Learson,

*"And what do you think I should tell Robbie
about selkies?"*

Yarl Corbie tossed the coin back among its fellows. "We'll have to leave them here," he said grimly,
"for even one of them taken ashore could trace this
night's doings back to us. And so weep no tears for
lost riches, my lad!"

Robbie took a resentful glance at him. "You'll
not catch *me* shedding tears for selkie gold," he declared. "And there's no need for you to tell me we
could buy nothing but trouble with it. I knew that
as soon as I guessed we would find it here."

"Well, well," said Yarl Corbie staring at this look
and the tone of voice that went with it. "You're quite
a spirited lad after all, it seems. But considering how
much is going to depend on you on Up Helly Aa,
that's just as well—isn't it?"

Turning on his heel then, he marched out of the

cave carrying the skin, and Robbie followed him down to the boat wondering what this last remark had meant. Once started on the return journey, too, he felt his curiosity about it growing sharper with every stroke of the oars; but when at last he did venture a question on it, Yarl Corbie told him curtly,

"It's too soon to talk about that. But this much I can tell you. Before we part tonight, I'll give you some of the instructions you'll need to carry out your part on Up Helly Aa. Tomorrow—once you're sure you haven't been missed from home this past hour or so—I'll give you the rest of these instructions. And meanwhile, the important thing for us is to find some other hiding place for the selkie skin."

"That's true," agreed Robbie, his thoughts flashing to other caves he had seen in other geos. "But where *can* we hide it?"

"Nowhere at sea," said Yarl Corbie, as if guessing these thoughts, "because that is the first place Finn Learson would search for it. Nowhere on land, because that is the second place he would search. We will hide it in a place that belongs neither to the sea nor to the land, a place that is open to every eye, but secret from all; a place which Finn Learson may enter as a man, yet which he cannot leave again except as the Great Selkie."

Robbie stopped rowing to peer at the hunched figure opposite him.

"There's no such place," he said wonderingly. "How can there be?"

Yarl Corbie made no answer to this, and after Robbie began rowing again, he continued to sit in silence. The boat grounded at last on the home beach. Together they drew it on to the shingle. Then, still without another word spoken between them, Yarl Corbie took Robbie to the place where he meant to hide the skin.

14

Nicol Promises

Robbie was up late the next morning, what with all the hours of sleep the business of the sealskin had cost him. Breakfast was over by the time he showed face in the but end, but nobody said a word in question of this—which made it certain, he decided, that he had not been missed from his bed the previous night.

Quietly, he helped himself to oatcakes and butter. Then, still fighting sleep, he sat munching his late breakfast and trying to remember everything about the instructions Yarl Corbie had given him on their way home from hiding the sealskin.

All the rest of the family, meanwhile, sat around talking and taking their ease on the first day of the holidays, with all of them having turns at telling Finn Learson what these would be like.

"It's a great time of the year, and no mistake," Peter remarked; and Janet agreed,

"Aye, you'll have your fill of dancing these holidays, Finn Learson, for the whole of Yule night is one big celebration, and it's the same at New Year and Up Helly Aa."

"Besides which," Peter added, "you'll see something to surprise you at the end of it all, for Up Helly Aa is also the night when all the young men go from house to house dressed up in a sort of disguise, with white handkerchiefs tied like masks over their faces."

"What's the reason for that?" Finn Learson asked, but Peter could not give any proper answer to this question.

"It's just a custom," he said vaguely. " 'Guising,' they call it, and the young fellows that dress up are the 'guisers.' "

Robbie came awake with a jerk then, for it was this very custom of guising, as it happened, which was at the heart of Yarl Corbie's instructions. Moreover, he realized, Finn Learson was clearly interested in it.

"And how do these guisers dress up?" he was asking. "What do they wear?"

"Petticoats!" Peter answered, laughing. "Long petticoats made of straw, with tall, pointed hats of straw, white shirts, and everything all covered with bunches of colored ribbons. That's how daft they look—and it's a daft name they have, too, for the one that leads all this foolery. The Skuddler, they call him, and you never *saw* such a wild dance as he commands from all the other guisers!"

"It sounds like an old custom to me; a very old custom," Finn Learson remarked: and immediately, the warning note in Robbie's mind sounded louder than ever. Quickly he rose and made for the door, but he was not to get away so easily as all that.

"Aye, I'm sure I've heard Old Da say as much," Peter was agreeing. "But it's Robbie you would need to ask about such things, for he was always the one that took in everything Old Da said about them."

Robbie had the door open by this time, but Peter's words had brought every eye to him, and so he still had to answer.

"I don't know any more than my Da," he mumbled to Finn Learson. Then out he dashed before the guilty flush on his face could betray that this was a lie; for fine he could remember Old Da talking to him of the Skuddler and his men. Fine he could remember Old Da saying there was an ancient magic behind their guising, and explaining the meaning of this magic to him.

Even so, he excused the lie to himself, he dared not disobey any of Yarl Corbie's instructions. And the very first of these had been that Finn Learson must not be allowed to guess the least thing about the magic or its meaning! Running quickly, Robbie made good his escape from the house. The next of

Yarl Corbie's instructions went through his mind as he ran, and straightaway, he headed off in search of Nicol Anderson. Nor did he waste a moment in coming to the point with Nicol, once he had managed to track him down that morning.

"There's a favor I want to ask of you, Nicol," he began. "If it comes to a fight between you and Finn Learson at Up Helly Aa, I want you to promise me the fight will take place above high-water mark."

Nicol stared at this. "I'll not let Elspeth go without a fight," he said. "That's one thing I *can* promise you. But what has high-water mark to do with it?"

"Everything," Robbie told him. "Finn Learson is a creature of the sea, and so all his power comes from the sea. But all that lies above high-water mark belongs to the land, and so that is where you will be the stronger of the two."

"So that's it!" Nicol exclaimed. "You're still on about this nonsense of the Great Selkie!"

"Yes, I am," Robbie told him defiantly. "But I'm not asking anymore for you to believe it. I just want you to do this as a favor for me. And there can't be any harm in that, surely?"

"No, I don't suppose there is," Nicol agreed. "It's just daft, that's all. But still, if it means so much to you—all right, Robbie. I'll fight him above high-water mark."

Robbie gave a sigh of relief. "Then there's just one more thing I want to ask," said he. "It's about the Skuddler, Nicol; and what I want to know is this. Which of you fellows will play the part at this year's Up Helly Aa?"

"That's a stupid question, isn't it?" Nicol demanded. "You know we always keep that a secret among ourselves."

"Of course I do," Robbie admitted. "But there's another favor I want of you."

Quickly then, but choosing his words so that Nicol could not guess who had prompted them, he went on to ask what Yarl Corbie had told him to ask. Nicol's face grew more and more puzzled as he listened, but at the end of it, he said,

"I suppose I could manage that—provided all the other fellows agree, of course."

"Will you fix it with them, then?" Robbie pressed. "Will you, Nicol?"

Nicol frowned. "Why should I?" he asked. "You haven't given me any reason for it, have you?"

"No," Robbie admitted. "But I don't want Elspeth to choose Finn Learson any more than you do, and I know this will give you the power to save her."

"You'll have to do better than that," Nicol remarked, "for that just doesn't make sense to me."

"It does to me," Robbie told him swiftly. "My Old Da explained everything about the guising to me, and so I know it makes sense."

"Your Old Da," said Nicol, "was a story-teller!

And so how could you tell whether he was speaking the truth about that, or whether it was just something he had made up?"

Robbie thought of Yarl Corbie talking to him as they walked home from hiding the sealskin. There was an easy answer to Nicol's question, he realized. *Because Yarl Corbie told me it was the truth.* Nicol would have to believe him then, for no one could doubt Yarl Corbie's knowledge of such matters. But then, also, what would become of his own promise to keep silent about Yarl Corbie?

"Old Da wasn't making up any story about the guising," he said at last. "I know I'm right in that, although I can't tell you how I do know. And if you do as I ask, Nicol, I *know* it will give you power against Finn Learson."

Nicol stared at him. "You really do believe all that nonsense about the Great Selkie," he said. "You're convinced of it, aren't you, Robbie?"

"You know I am," said Robbie, biting his lip. "And I really do believe Elspeth is in danger from him. Which makes it very hard when you won't even take a chance on doing something to save her."

Nicol hesitated, seemingly quite impressed by these last words, and Robbie rushed in to take advantage of this hesitation.

"Please!" he begged. "For old times' sake, Nicol."

Nicol suddenly made up his mind. "All right," he agreed, and even managed a smile on the words.

"If that's what it really takes to put your mind at ease, I'll fix it with the other fellows—for old times' sake, Robbie!"

Once more, Robbie sighed in relief. "Fine, man! Fine!" he exclaimed. "And don't forget what I said about high-water mark. Keep above that mark on Up Helly Aa, *and be sure you keep Elspeth above it, too.*"

Nicol smiled again, as if the whole idea had really begun to amuse him now that he had given in to it at last. His smile broadened, until his face was like the big laughing sun it used to be before Finn Learson came into his life; and clapping Robbie on the shoulder, he remarked,

"I'll say this for you, Robbie Henderson. I never met a lad with such a determined streak in him as you have! Besides which, even your Old Da never had such a wild imagination as yours!"

Robbie laughed, thinking he did not care what anyone said of him now that he had got Nicol to fall in with Yarl Corbie's plan.

"We'll see who's right about all this when Up Helly Aa comes!" he retorted, and took his leave of Nicol feeling he could hardly wait for this to happen.

It was not towards home he turned, however, but towards the schoolhouse; and he went roundabout, so that no one would realize he was headed there. Cautiously he knocked on the door of Yarl Corbie's own but-and-ben, and when the door was opened to him, he slipped in as quiet as a shadow.

"Did anyone see you come here?" Yarl Corbie shot at him.

Robbie shook his head. "I came round the back of the hill," he explained. "And it doesn't seem as if I was missed from home last night, either."

"Good!" Yarl Corbie told him. "And what about Nicol Anderson?"

"I've spoken to him," Robbie answered triumphantly, "and he's promised to do what you want on Up Helly Aa."

"But you didn't let him guess that *I* was behind the idea, did you?" Yarl Corbie asked.

"No," Robbie told him. "I put it to Nicol exactly the way you said I should."

Yarl Corbie rubbed his hands and went back to sit in his chair by the fire. "That's fine!" he declared. "That means nobody can possibly guess I'm mixed up in this, and so now I can really plan. Come here, boy!"

15

Yarl Corbie Plans

Robbie went over to stand beside Yarl Corbie's chair, but he moved unwillingly, for he had never been inside the schoolmaster's house before, and he could see things there which made him uneasy.

There was a human skull standing on the window-sill, for instance, and this skull seemed to be grinning at him. From the rafters above his head, dangled bunches of dried herbs that gave off a peculiar, musty odor. A book lay open on the table, a big book with pages so yellow in color that he guessed it must be very old.

Moreover, these yellowish pages were covered with writing that was all back-to-front—mirror writing, in fact, and he remembered Old Da had told him this was the kind of writing wizards used for their spells!

"Closer, boy, closer!" Yarl Corbie said impatiently. "Walls have ears, they say, and this is only for the two of us to hear."

Obediently Robbie came closer, then gasped, as Yarl Corbie shot out a large hand to grip his arm. In growing fear he looked down at the dark and beaky face upturned to him, and Yarl Corbie grinned at the expression he wore.

"You're still frightened of me," he said softly. "And that's good. It means you'll continue to keep your mouth shut about me, doesn't it?"

For the life of him, Robbie could not say a word then. He simply nodded, and Yarl Corbie went on,

"Now listen. The important thing for you to do on Up Helly Aa, is to *keep Elspeth in sight*. Where she goes, Finn Learson will go—depend on that; and so you must never take your eyes off her."

"But she'll be visiting back and forward to all the neighbors, the way everyone does then," Robbie protested. "I could easily lose sight of her in the darkness when that happens."

"If you do," said Yarl Corbie grimly, "you'll lose her altogether, for you won't be there when Finn Learson tempts her away with him."

Robbie thought of how very dark it would be in the dark hours of Up Helly Aa, and in spite of himself, he began to shake.

"The trows will be out on Up Helly Aa," he whispered, "and you know it's on that night they have their greatest power. Supposing I meet with some of *them* when I'm trying to keep Elspeth in sight?"

"You'll do as your Old Da taught you," Yarl Corbie told him. "You'll cross yourself and say the words they hate to hear."

Robbie stared in dismay at this, for *nobody* dared to go out alone on Up Helly Aa however much they were blessed against the power of the trows. Moreover, he remembered, it was always young folk like himself that were in special danger of being stolen away to the strange, secret mounds where they had their homes. Yarl Corbie was still talking, however, and so he had to force himself to listen.

"The next thing for you to remember," Yarl Corbie was saying, "is this. *Only the Skuddler can save Elspeth*; and so, the moment that Finn Learson acts, you must act too. You must find the Skuddler. Also, if anything happens to make Nicol fall short of the part *we* hope he will play, remember that you still have the knowledge which will give you the whip-hand over Finn Learson; for only you can tell him that his selkie skin is in a different hiding-place, and only you can lead him to it."

"But if I go alone with him to that place," said Robbie in even deeper dismay now, "there won't be anyone to stop him getting the skin back and then doing what he likes with me."

"Yes, there will," Yarl Corbie told him. "*I* will be there."

"And you won't let him harm me?" Robbie asked fearfully.

Yarl Corbie loosed his grip on Robbie's arm, and

rose to his full, lean height. His eyes went to the table and the book of mirror writing lying there, and softly he said,

"I've already told you I want my revenge on Finn Learson, and now I have found the very spell to let me do that. And so now also, you can be sure of one thing. When Finn Learson comes out of that place where the skin is hidden, he will not be able to harm anyone, ever again."

Robbie backed a step. "Why?" he asked fearfully. "What—what kind of a spell is it?"

"One that I mean to be as big a surprise to you as it will be to him," Yarl Corbie answered, lifting his eyes from the book to let them rest on Robbie. "And now, until Up Helly Aa that is *all* I have to say to you."

There was something so cruel in Yarl Corbie's look then, that Robbie was much relieved to hear this. Nervously he backed even further; and once again, as soon as he was out of the door, he made for home with all the speed he could muster.

His mother was baking when he got there, and the house was full of the smell of freshly made Yule bannocks. Elspeth was at the byre door, hanging up a charm to protect the cattle from the power of the trows at Yule, and he went obediently to help her with this when his mother told him to do so.

Robbie's heart was not in this matter, however. Nor could he take an interest in any of the things that had always before made the Yule holidays so exciting for him. All he could think of now, in fact, was the end of the holidays and Up Helly Aa, so that all the days before then began to take on the feelings of days passing in a long and seemingly endless dream.

There was one thing, however, which stood out from the dream in which Robbie now moved, and this was the change that each of these passing days seemed to work on Nicol and Elspeth.

Nicol, of course, had been growing steadily more sullen before that time; but gradually now, he became so grim and scowling that people could hardly believe he had once been a cheerful, easy-going man. Elspeth, too, no longer laughed or sang as she went around the house; and the quieter she became, the more often her eyes took on a certain trance-like look that made her seem like a sleep-walker wandering about in broad daylight.

It seemed to Robbie too, that the times this trance came over her were always those when her eyes met Finn Learson's gaze. And then, he noticed, Finn Learson would smile his secret little smile. For a moment, also, the young and handsome appearance of his face would slip aside like a mask, and another face would look out at Elspeth—a watchful, old, and cunning face that held her fascinated, the way Tam had been held fascinated on Finn Learson's first night in the house.

A great dread of these moments began to creep

over Robbie, and very often he wondered why everyone else was so blind to everything that seemed so clear to himself. The truth of the matter, however, was still so far from every mind except his own, that no one saw anything at all remarkable in the situation.

Nicol's grimness and sulking, they argued, was simply due to jealousy. A young girl like Elspeth, with such a decision ahead of her, was bound to be absent-minded. As for Finn Learson, everyone continued to find him so pleasant and polite that they could hardly be expected to guess at the uncanny presence lurking behind the charm of his manner. It was quite the opposite case, in fact, for none of them could fail to mark that he quite put Nicol to shame with the way he refused to be upset by Elspeth's decision about waiting for the end of Up Helly Aa to make her choice between them.

At the Christmas and New Year celebrations he danced with her as light-heartedly as he had ever done. Nicol, on the other hand, sat scowling in a corner without even trying to persuade her to partner him; and this led Janet to speak up quite sharply, for she still had a soft spot in her heart for Nicol. Besides which, as she had now begun to realize, the debt that she and Peter owed Finn Learson did not mean she was really happy to see their daughter wedded to a foreign man who would very likely take her back with him to his own country. And so, by the time it came to the New Year, she was ready to tell Nicol.

"That's no way to get Elspeth to decide in your favor—sitting there with a long face on you while the other fellow does all the courting!"

"Aye, you'll have to stir yourself if you really want to win her," Peter added to this remark; but Nicol remained stubborn.

"I courted Elspeth before Finn Learson came," he argued, "and I've courted her since then—well enough to let her know I would be good to her and she would be happy with me. Now she must decide for herself without me running after her and staring into her eyes the way *he* does."

On the early evening of Up Helly Aa, however, Nicol showed a different spirit, for he came to the house then, with a present of scarlet ribbons for Elspeth to tie in her hair. Janet, by this time, had set out food and drink for all the neighbors who would visit. Peter had tuned his fiddle. Elspeth had brushed her golden hair until the rippling shine of it was a dazzle to the eye; and staring greedily at this, Finn Learson told her,

"You look like a princess."

Elspeth blushed to hear him speak so; and just at the moment that Nicol entered the house, Finn Learson added boldly,

"And when you marry me, you will be princess of my whole kingdom."

Peter and Janet smiled at this, taking it to be no

more than a piece of romantic nonsense, but Robbie knew differently. *The kingdom under the sea,* he thought in horror; and in his mind's eye he saw Elspeth's face among the faces of all the other golden-haired girls who had once reigned as the Great Selkie's princess—the girls who had tried to escape, the drowned girls . . .

"I've brought you a present, Elspeth," Nicol's voice broke into these thoughts, and Robbie watched him holding the scarlet ribbons out to her. She took them, smiling and exclaiming over their color, and immediately began twisting them through the shining strands of her hair. For one wild moment then, Robbie thought all his troubles might be ended, for the way Elspeth looked at Nicol when she had done this seemed to show that *he* was the one she really wanted to choose. Nicol gave her look for look, and quietly he said,

"I cannot make fine speeches the way *he* does, Elspeth. I have never learned such manners. But this I will say with all my heart. I will hold you tonight if he tries to take you from me, *and I will never let you go from that hold.*"

"Nicol!" said Elspeth, with all her soul in her voice. "Oh, Nicol!" And then Finn Learson laughed, spoiling the moment for all of them.

"You speak brave words," he told Nicol contemptuously. "But you have still to prove them, and the night is not out yet."

"No more it is!" exclaimed Peter, taking up his fiddle to cover the awkwardness he felt, for it looked then and there as if it would come to a fight between the other two; but Nicol turned on his heel, and it was Finn Learson who danced with Elspeth then.

Robbie watched Nicol stride from the house, knowing that Elspeth's last chance to declare for him had gone and that everything now depended on himself—and on the Skuddler. Grimly then, he settled down to await the appearance of the guisers, crouching in a corner with his hands twined in Tam's fur and his eyes constantly marking the time on the grandfather clock.

The guisers would be visiting every house in Black Ness that night, he knew, and so it would be well after midnight before he could expect to see them. Yet still he rushed to open the door every time he heard footsteps and voices outside the house; and each time, he was disappointed to find it was only more neighbors arriving.

Tam became restless, whining and shivering uneasily, and he wondered if the creature could sense what would happen that night. The hands of the clock seemed to move so slowly that sometimes he thought they had stopped altogether. He stayed alert, all the same, and at one o'clock in the morning when the guisers came at last, he was at the door before anyone else could reach it.

Flinging it wide open, he saw the whole mob of them standing outside. The next moment, they were all around him; and from somewhere in the mob, a voice—Nicol's voice—breathed in his ear,

"All right, Robbie! I've fixed it!"

And so there was hope yet for Elspeth, Robbie thought triumphantly. Then, with his heart beating hard in the excitement of this moment, he was carried back into the room by the rushing entrance of the Skuddler and the Skuddler's men.

16

Guisers

There were twenty-six of the guisers, all told. Their long straw petticoats and high, pointed hats made them all seem taller than ordinary men. The bunches of colored ribbons tied on petticoats, hats, and shirts were like curiously shaped fruit and flowers sprouting everywhere from them. The eyes above their handkerchief masks looked out like the eyes of mysterious strangers. Like strangers, too, they entered in deadly silence; for—as Robbie had just proved—even a few words spoken could give away the secret behind the mask.

A shout of greeting went up at the sight of them, and everyone rose so that there would be room for them to dance. Chairs were pushed back against the walls. Peter raised his fiddle; and still without a word spoken, the Skuddler's men formed a circle with the Skuddler himself at its center.

Peter struck an opening chord. The Skuddler

raised the long white wand he carried in his right hand. Peter swung into a fast-stepping reel, and with a swish of his wand, the Skuddler commanded the dance to begin.

Instantly then, the but end seemed to explode into a whirling mass of straw. Tall hats shot up and down like tongues of flame flickering through the mass. Colored ribbons tossed about in it, like fruit falling, like flowers being torn off in a gale.

The watchers in the but end clapped in time to the dancers' antics. They cheered, they laughed. They shouted out guesses about which face lay behind which mask. For all the wildness of this dance, however, it was still carried on in deadly silence. It was still under the Skuddler's command, too, for it was his wand that continued to direct all its movements.

Up and down the dancers leaped. In and out they wove. Round and about they whirled and twisted, all in obedience to the wand. The signals from it divided them into pairs, into larger groups, and then brought them back into one mass. Another signal stilled all the others while each man danced alone; and as he danced, each and every man kept his eyes on the wand. Each and every man danced for the Skuddler, but the Skuddler himself never shifted position.

It was only the hand with the wand in it that moved. And his eyes! The eyes of the Skuddler were everywhere, darting from dancer to dancer; and away at the back of his mind as he watched this, Robbie heard once more the voice of his Old Da explaining to him the dance of the Skuddler's men.

"They are supposed to be earth spirits—the spirits of corn, and fruit, and flowers—and the Skuddler himself is the god of the earth commanding them to dance in honor of all the good things he has created. . . ."

"What's the meaning of it all?" a voice breathed in Robbie's ear, and turning towards the sound, he met the gaze of big, dark eyes—Finn Learson's eyes drawing him into the same circle of mysterious power that held Tam and Elspeth; Finn Learson guessing at the knowledge Old Da had passed on and probing his mind for the secret of it.

"I don't know," Robbie lied, trying hard to break away from the gaze; but the voice of Old Da was still running through his mind, and he was desperately afraid that Finn Learson could somehow also hear it saying,

"It was the way they made magic in old heathen times, Robbie. The dressing-up was a sort of spell. The dancing was another part of the spell, and the whole thing made a magic that turned them into the creatures they were supposed to be—the earth-god and his spirits. . . ."

"Who's playing the Skuddler?" Finn Learson demanded. "Do you know *that*?"

Robbie backed off from the eyes boring into his own, then found that he had backed into his mother, and sighed with relief to hear her answering for him.

"Nobody knows," she told Finn Learson. "The young men always decide that among themselves, and it won't be until they all unmask at the end of Up Helly Aa that *we* learn which of them it is."

A burst of cheering and clapping from all around announced the sudden end of the dance. Robbie found himself once more surrounded by the guisers as they crowded to take their share of the food and drink laid out. Shouts of laughter came from people jostling to watch each one swallow as much as he could without lifting more than a corner of his mask. Then Peter's fiddle shrilled out again.

The Skuddler's men swept back on to the dancing space, each with a partner from among the guests. Another fiddler joined Peter's efforts, and yet another. The but end became a wild, weaving whirl of figures stamping in time to the music. The laughing faces of girls bobbed about among the white-masked faces of the guisers. Peter and the other two fiddlers stood perched above the dancers, their faces red and shining with sweat, their bows racing back and forth at mad speed across the fiddle-strings.

Somebody seized Robbie's hand and pulled him into the whirl of dancers. He caught the gleam of white teeth and dark eyes as Finn Learson spun by, laughing, with Janet on his arm. A tall figure loomed over him, a masked face looked down, and the grim eyes of the Skuddler met his own. Briefly he glimpsed Elspeth's hair in a tangle of gold, and scarlet ribbons, and then he was too dizzy to be aware of anything else except the floor heaving under his feet and the roof rafters seeming to turn like the spokes of a huge wheel above his head.

A gust of cold night air and a last ringing chord from the fiddles brought him to himself. Somebody had opened the door, he realized. The dance was at an end, and the guisers were departing to visit the next house on their rounds. Silent to the last, they were beginning to vanish through the doorway, waving farewells as they went, and all the younger folk among the guests were jostling to follow them.

Robbie was still dizzy. He held on to a chair to steady himself, and to his dismay, saw that Finn Learson and Elspeth were among those following in the wake of the Skuddler and his men. Quickly, in case his father or mother saw him leave, he ducked low and slid neatly in among the jostling throng.

The next moment he was outside and catching his breath in wonder at what he saw there, for there was a strange, tingling feeling in the air, and instead of the velvety darkness he had expected, the whole sky was aflame with green, leaping light.

Somebody shouted, *"It's the Merry Dancers!"*— which is the name they have in these parts for the peculiar lights that sometimes leap and flicker over northern skies in winter—and this cry was taken up on all sides, for nobody could think when they had last seen so fine a display of these northern lights.

Every face stared upwards, and everyone began turning round and around as they stared, for the light seemed sometimes to roll in great green waves over the sky, and sometimes it was like long search-lights of green shooting brilliantly out from a huge and starless black dome. Sometimes too, all the green would vanish for a few seconds, and everybody was blinded by darkness until the lights appeared again, in little tongues of leaping, dancing green flame.

Robbie stared upwards with the rest, all thought of Elspeth suddenly forgotten in his wonder at this sky. Then, too late, he realized that the Skuddler and his men had moved on, and the others were following in little groups that straggled all over the hillside.

Shouting, he ran to catch up with the nearest of these groups, then stopped in sudden terror that they might be trows, for part of the power trows have at Up Helly Aa is that they can take on any shape they wish. Yet still, he reminded himself, he *had* to keep track of Finn Learson and Elspeth. He simply had to! In a shaking voice he mumbled,

"God be about me and all that I see." Then, hastily he crossed himself, and stumbled on; but it still did not prove easy to find Finn Learson and Elspeth among all those straggling groups, and with every hour after that, Robbie found it growing still harder to keep on their trail.

At the next house, the Skuddler and his band departed without any train of followers; but still there were people visiting back and forth between all the houses scattered over the hill, for in every house that night there was light, and music, and celebration of some kind. Moreover, Elspeth was as footloose as any of the others roaming the hill; and in each house she and Finn Learson visited, Robbie seemed to find himself being caught up in the celebrations at the very moment these two were ready to leave for some other place.

In one house, it was a guessing game that held him trapped among boys of his own age, all clustering around him to shout the riddle,

> *Wingle wangle, like a tangle,*
> *If I was even, I'd reach to Heaven.*

The more he tried to free himself too, the louder they called, "What am I? Guess, Robbie Henderson, guess!"

But still Robbie could not guess—until Elspeth herself gave him the clue. Turning at the doorway with Finn Learson, she smiled good-bye at everyone there; and in a flash, Robbie remembered her footprint in the *lik* straw, and the tangle of smoke uncoiling slowly out towards the summer sky.

"Smoke!" Triumphantly he shouted the answer, and darted outside to follow the two figures dancing and running on their way under the green lights of the Merry Dancers.

In another house it was a dance that held him marooned in a corner while Elspeth disappeared. In yet another house he was helping to hand around the food when she decided to move on, and he had no choice but to drop a plate of scones to the floor while he dashed after her. Yet still, in spite of all such problems, he had to make sure Finn Learson did not notice how closely he was keeping on Elspeth's trail, and a dozen times that night he blessed Nicol for the scarlet hair-ribbons that picked her out from all the other people milling around.

The further the night went on, however, the more difficult he found it to keep her always under his eye; for the further the night went on, of course, the more tired he grew. His legs began to ache with running over the tough, springy grass of the hill. His eyes smarted from lack of sleep, and it was the smarting eyes which at last betrayed him.

One moment he had the will-o'-the-wisp figure of Elspeth full in view as she danced ahead of him across the hill. The next moment, his weary eyelids drooped, and before he could blink them open again, the green of the northern lights had vanished behind one of the sky's spells of total darkness.

17

The Skuddler

A blind man would have been better off than Robbie at that moment, for a blind man could at least have used his other senses to aid him. Robbie was so panic-stricken, however, that he could not even judge the direction of the voices echoing faintly back to him; and by the time the green glow rolled over the sky again, the figures he had been following were too far off for him to say exactly which house they were making for, or which one of them was Elspeth.

He would just have to make for the nearest house, he decided then, for that would be the likeliest place to find her; and off he went, running as hard as he could towards a gleam of yellow lamplight beckoning across the hill. But no, he was told when he reached this house, Elspeth was not there.

"Try Laurie Tulloch's house," someone advised him; and so off he went again, only to find that this had also been a wild-goose chase.

"Try Bruce Hunter's house," he was told, when he started asking then if anyone knew where Elspeth had last been headed, and wearily Robbie turned in that direction. But now it was no longer a case of running fast, for he was nearly dropping with exhaustion by this time.

He ran a few steps, he walked a few steps, then ran again. And now also, he realized, he was by no means alone on the hill, for wherever he turned his eyes he seemed to catch glimpses of figures outlined darkly against the green sky—weird figures that ran or danced or gestured strangely—and the fear of trows grew so strong on him that he did not dare to wave or call or do anything which would draw their attention to himself.

His right arm seemed to be powerless, too, for—try as he would—he could not lift it to bless himself. Moreover, the words that trows hate to hear seemed to have vanished from his mind. In panic at this, he tried to run faster, but like someone in a waking nightmare, he found that his feet had become ton weights and that he could no longer trust his own senses.

He heard laughter crackling faintly on the still, night air. He saw the strange figures draw nearer, then vanish suddenly, and reappear in different places. They loomed large against the night-sky. They grew small again, small as trows! Robbie ran on—slowly, slowly, his breath sobbing in ever-growing terror, yet still not knowing whether all this was really happening, or whether it was only the strange green sky and the hill's uneven outline that were playing tricks on his sight.

One thing he did know, however, and with the utmost despair he admitted this to himself. He had now completely lost track of Elspeth; and so now the only purpose in his running was to escape all those weird figures that threatened him, and then somehow to find the Skuddler.

Another sound broke on his hearing, a sound much louder than the occasional crackle of laughter. It came from the seashore—from the beach down at the voe—and instantly he knew what it was, for once before he had heard that same sound. It was Tam howling, he realized. Somewhere down at the voe Tam was howling the same long-drawn-out cry of mourning he had raised at the moment of Old Da's death.

For all his terror then, Robbie stopped dead in his tracks. There could be only one reason for that cry, he told himself. Finn Learson and Elspeth must be down at the voe at that very moment; and Tam was there too—howling for Elspeth's last moments on earth!

The thought of this hit Robbie with a shock that was like cold water dashed on his face. He gasped, feeling his brain clearing on the instant and the power coming back into his right arm. Quickly he blessed himself and called aloud the words that trows hate to hear; and like black shadows snuffed out by the sun, the leaping figures on the hillside disappeared.

Or so it seemed for the moment, anyway, but a second look showed Robbie that some of the figures were still running along the skyline of a ridge above the point where he stood. They were peculiarly shaped figures, too, but now that he had his courage back he could tell who they were.

For a moment, Robbie turned from them to look down towards the voe. A boat rocked there at the water's edge. Two forms stood on the beach above the boat. Some distance from the forms, a dog crouched, mournfully howling. Robbie took a deep breath, then he faced about towards the line of running figures, and yelled,

"Skuddler! Sku-u-u-dd-ler!"

The figures stumbled to a halt. They turned to the sound of his voice, and stood poised on the ridge. Now they looked like a row of haystacks planted there, their long petticoats billowing round them, their tall hats poking the sky. Robbie drew in another lungful of breath, and yelled again,

"Sku-u-u-dd-ler!"

One figure broke from the line and came plunging towards him. Robbie turned and ran ahead of it, shouting back over his shoulder as he ran,

"Finn Learson, Skuddler, Finn Learson! Down there—look! He's going off with Elspeth!"

The tall form of the Skuddler overtook Robbie, and thundered ahead of him towards the beach; but Robbie was not far behind, and the closer he drew to the beach, the more clearly he could see what was happening there. Finn Learson had Elspeth by the hand. His arm was outstretched, as if he were trying to pull her or coax her nearer the boat at the water's edge. But Tam was still at his mournful howling, and Elspeth was hanging back like someone frightened to take another step.

"Let her go!" the Skuddler roared, and Elspeth began struggling to snatch her hand from Finn Learson's grip.

The Skuddler roared again, and with a flying leap that took him on to the shingle of the beach, he seized her other hand. Elspeth screamed, a loud scream of fear and pain—and small wonder, either, for now she was stretched out between him and Finn Learson, with each of them determined to pull her from the other.

"You'll kill her!" yelled Robbie, for no one knew better than himself, then, that the magic behind the guising had turned the Skuddler into the earth-god he was supposed to be. And how could anyone live, pulled like that between all the forces of earth-magic and sea-magic?

"I'll kill him first!" the Skuddler roared, and made a sudden lunge that let him circle Elspeth's waist with one arm. The movement took Finn Learson by surprise. He stumbled, and in the flash of time it took for this, his grip slackened enough to let Elspeth snatch her hand free.

One swinging movement of the Skuddler's arm took her out of Finn Learson's reach. With Elspeth behind him then, the Skuddler backed away up the shingle, but Finn Learson shouted with rage, and leaped forward to close with him. Tam dashed for cover. Elspeth sank, weeping, to her knees, and Robbie edged as close as he could to the two forms swaying back and forth across the shingle.

Both men were panting now, their bodies locked in a hating embrace as each tried for a hold that would bring the other down; but Finn Learson's rush at the Skuddler had carried the fight above high-water mark, and with feelings of dreadful joy, Robbie saw the result this was having.

The Skudder was big enough already, for he was a tall man and his high, pointed hat made him even taller. But now, to Robbie's eyes, he seemed to grow bigger and more powerful with every moment that passed. And Finn Learson was also changing!

Finn Learson was aging, it seemed to Robbie. The skin of his face was withering, falling away into wrinkles. His hands were becoming an old man's hands—stringy, with muscles bunched like badly tied knots. The youthful lines of his body were sagging into something twisted, and evil, and very, very old.

The movement of the Skuddler's long legs set his

straw petticoats flailing like a harvest field struck by storm. His wide shoulders seemed to grow even wider in a heave of terrible effort to break the grip of the stringy old hands. The tall cone of his hat towered even higher against the green-lit sky. The white mask beneath the hat loomed ever more threatening and mysterious over Finn Learson's aging face; and with a final tremendous heave, the Skuddler brought him to the ground.

"Watch out!" shouted Robbie then, for the two of them had fallen right across the high-water mark. The shout brought Elspeth to his side, crying out in fear and trying to hold him back as he made to dash towards the two struggling figures. But Robbie was too desperate to be held at that moment.

"The high-water mark!" he yelled, wrenching himself free of Elspeth's hands. "Get him back over the high-water mark, Skuddler!"

The Skuddler knelt astride Finn Learson and gave a heave that was meant to lift him clear over the dry seaweed marking the highest point of the tide; but this movement freed one of Finn Learson's arms, and he was still half in his own territory—which meant he was not yet conquered.

The free hand came quickly up in a thrust that sent both himself and the Skuddler rolling over and over, and a horrified Robbie saw them coming to rest well below the high-water mark. Shouting, he ran after them, knowing that any moment now the time might come for *him* to act; for now they were in Finn Learson's territory where his sea-magic was bound to defeat the Skuddler's power.

"Robbie!" Elspeth screamed after him, "*Robbie!*" But he ran on, paying not the slightest heed to this.

It was Finn Learson who was on top in the struggle now—Finn Learson with all his youth and strength restored, Finn Learson kneeling over a Skuddler suddenly stripped of all the earth-god's power. One hand held the Skuddler down. The other hand was stretched out towards the white mask. A single jerk whipped the mask free, and a face stared up from the shingle—the flushed and angry face of Nicol Anderson.

Finn Learson breathed a long sigh of understanding. A grin of triumph spread over his face, and quick as a flash, he shot out both hands to Nicol's throat. Nicol gasped at their grip, and Robbie also gasped, for the deadly purpose of it was clear; and this was something he had not bargained for when he persuaded Nicol to fix it so that *he* played the part of the Skuddler.

Finn Learson squeezed still harder, and Robbie threw himself forward, clutching and tearing at the death-grip on Nicol's throat.

"Leave him!" he yelled. "Let him live—or you'll never see the Great Selkie's skin again!"

Finn Learson's head jerked up in astonishment, but his fingers were still gripping tight enough to choke Nicol, and Robbie hurried on,

"I've got your skin, Finn Learson. I stole it from the cave, and if you kill Nicol, I'll *never* tell where it is now!"

Slowly Finn Learson's hands loosened their grip. Slowly he rose, and standing astride of Nicol, he glared down at Robbie.

"What skin?" he challenged. "What fancy are you spinning now, Robbie Henderson?"

"This is no fancy," Robbie told him defiantly. "And it is no use pretending with me, for I *know* who you are and why you came ashore. That's why I stole your skin—and that's why you'll never get it back without me."

Finn Learson stepped clear of Nicol's body. "So you think you have the advantage of me now, do you?" he asked harshly. "Well, take me to this skin, boy, and then we shall see who really has the advantage!"

One powerful hand clamped down on Robbie's shoulder, keeping tight hold of him as he started forward in obedience to its urging. At the top of the beach, however, he managed to steal a backward glance that showed him Elspeth running to help Nicol to his feet, and Tam frisking beside her as she ran.

A first, small thrill of triumph shot through Robbie then, and feeling braver than he had imagined he would at that moment, he led on to the place where Yarl Corbie had hidden the Great Selkie's skin.

18

The Great Selkie

Nowhere at sea . . . That was what Yarl Corbie had
said, and that was why Robbie turned his back on
the voe when he walked away with Finn Learson's
hand on his shoulder. *Nowhere on land . . .* Yarl
Corbie had said, and so Robbie did not continue
walking inland. Instead, he took Finn Learson to the
top of the cliffs running west of the voe, seeing his
way by the light of the Merry Dancers, still flaring
green overhead.

For half a mile then, he led the way over the close,
thick turf clothing the rock of the clifftops, and this
brought them to a point where a great hole opened
suddenly in the turf-covered rock. The hole was
deep—deeper than any eye could guess or tell. Its
walls were sheer rock, and from somewhere at the
foot of those steep, rocky walls came the sound of
water swishing and swirling about.

Robbie halted at the lip of the hole, and there he

glanced around, fully expecting to see Yarl Corbie coming towards him. To his utmost dismay, however, there was no Yarl Corbie in sight and not even the slightest hint of his presence.

"We'll have to wait," he said desperately over his shoulder to Finn Learson. "I can't tell you yet where the skin is."

Finn Learson gave not a word in answer to this. He simply turned Robbie towards himself and that was answer enough; for it was then, Robbie realized, that he was seeing at last the true face of Finn the Magician.

In mortal terror at the sight, he shrank as far back as he could. The face hovered over him, and it was not old, or young, nor yet anything in between, but simply a shifting blur of features that changed with every nightmare moment of his stare at it. It was no face at all, in fact, and yet somehow it was still every face that had ever haunted his deepest fears and his darkest dreams.

The eyes of the faceless face bored into his own, for they were the one thing about the nightmare that did not change. They were still the great dark eyes which had tried to trap him earlier that night, and he could feel them probing his mind again, forcing him somehow to give away his knowledge of the hiding-place Yarl Corbie had found for the Great Selkie's skin.

In a shaking voice, Robbie began to speak of the

place that was open to every eye, and yet secret from all.

"This great hole beside us," said he, "is more than a hole, for it was made by the action of the sea boring a tunnel deep underground through a crack in the rock of the cliffs. And your skin is in the tunnel that leads from the hole."

Triumph flashed from the dark gaze holding him in its spell. The figure towering over him swung round towards the hole. It teetered at the edge, ready to plunge into the sea-water that sucked and swirled far below; and as it swayed there, a black shape rose swiftly up from the concealing darkness of a ledge a few feet down the rocky wall of the hole.

The shape became the form of a bird that called out with the croaking voice of a raven. A noise of great, dark wings flapping, mingled with its cry. The wings beat furiously around the head of the figure swaying on the edge of the hole. The figure cried out—a terrible cry of pain that was neither animal nor human. Then, with hands clapped to its eyes, it hurtled helplessly into the depths below.

The raven wheeled to flap in a circle around the place where Robbie stood, shaken out of his wits by this turn of events, and hurriedly he threw himself flat on the ground. Trembling, he lay there hugging his head with his arms and not knowing what to expect next. But nothing happened—nothing at all, and at last he ventured to raise his head again.

At first, he thought he was alone. The next instant he realized there was someone standing over him. He rolled away from the someone, ready to jump up and run for dear life, but he was hardly on his feet before he realized it was Yarl Corbie standing there.

Anger seized him then, and recklessly he shouted, "Where were *you* a minute ago? You promised to be here in time!"

"Where was I?" Yarl Corbie echoed. "Where do you think I was, boy? You came asking for magic to help you, and it is not for nothing I am nicknamed Yarl Corbie!"

Robbie backed a step, his mind spinning with thoughts of the mirror writing in Yarl Corbie's ancient book of spells and the raven that had flapped around the head of the falling figure.

"You . . . ?" he whispered. "You were that—*You* were the raven?"

"Why not?" Yarl Corbie asked coolly. "There was no better way to take him by surprise; and no better way, either, to have my revenge on him."

Robbie stared, still trying to take in the thought of Yarl Corbie transformed to the shape of a raven. The cry, the terrible cry of pain rang in his mind again. His gaze shifted to the black mouth of the hole, and Yarl Corbie chuckled, a dry and whispery sound that was more like a cough than a chuckle.

"You'll not see him come back out of there," he remarked, "—but you *will* be able to see him come out of the cave at the seaward end of the tunnel!"

Turning on his heel with this, he strode briskly away from the hole. Robbie hesitated to follow, but curiosity drove him on; and at the very edge of the cliffs, Yarl Corbie halted to wait for him.

"Watch there," said he, pointing downwards as Robbie drew level. "And wait for the next flash of the Merry Dancers."

Robbie stared down to the white foam and steely shimmer of the water at the cliff-foot. The Merry Dancers were still flickering over the sky but their light was too faint to show him anything more than this, and impatiently he looked up to wait for their next flash.

"Keep your eyes down," Yarl Corbie warned.

There was a few moments of silence after that; and then suddenly, the flash came. It was a brilliant one, too, lighting up sea and sky like a great green searchlight; and right in the searchlight's path across the water, they saw what they had been waiting for— the head of a great bull seal forging rapidly seawards.

"There he goes!" Robbie shouted.

"Aye, there he goes," Yarl Corbie echoed. "But he'll go back to his own country a different creature from the one that came out of it!"

Robbie glanced up in wonder at the tall figure beside him. "Why did he cry out like that?" he asked. "What did you *do* to him?"

Yarl Corbie gave another of his dry, whispery

chuckles. "A raven's beak is a powerful weapon," he said softly, "—powerful enough to blind a man. And that was the revenge I chose to have!"

Robbie felt a shiver of horror running over him. "But a selkie hunts with its eyes," he exclaimed. "And so you might as well say you've doomed him to starve to death!"

"Would that be so bad?" Yarl Corbie asked.

"I don't know," Robbie admitted. "But it's cruel, all the same."

Yarl Corbie shrugged. "The thought does you credit, I suppose," he said drily. "But my revenge was neater than that—much neater! I blinded him of only *one* eye—which means he will still be able to hunt the seas the way a selkie does, but never again will he be able to come ashore in the shape of a handsome young man. And so never again will he have the chance to hunt human quarry!"

Robbie's gaze went back to the great dark head traveling seawards. It *was* a neat revenge, he admitted to himself—cruel, but neat; for certainly the Great Selkie would no longer be able to charm golden-haired girls like Elspeth when he could no longer be handsome in human form!

The light on the water went out as Robbie stared. Yarl Corbie turned him homewards, and that was the very last sight he had of the Great Selkie. Or so it seemed at that time, at least, for he had no cause then to think otherwise.

"And it is the very last you are to speak of him, too, remember," Yarl Corbie reminded him as they walked back along the cliffs. "For if one word of my part in this gets out in Black Ness, Robbie Henderson, I'll know where it came from. And you've just seen how I take revenge on those who harm me!"

"I know," said Robbie, shivering with remembered horror. "You don't ever have to fear that *I'll* run foul of you!"

The way things turned out after that, however, there was never any danger of Robbie mentioning either his own or Yarl Corbie's part in the whole business, for there was still nobody else who found anything mysterious about it. Indeed, so far as everyone else was concerned, the story was still a perfectly simple one—the sort of thing that could have happened anywhere, in fact.

A stranger had come ashore to Black Ness, and there he had fallen in love with Elspeth Henderson. Then there had been a fight between him and Elspeth's young man, and the stranger had taken off in the huff. That was how everyone saw things when Finn Learson did not appear the next morning, and for many years afterwards, that was what everyone continued to believe.

Peter and Janet Henderson never did learn the truth, in fact, since Yarl Corbie outlived them both, and Robbie dared not speak out so long as *he* was alive. So the years went past, with Elspeth and Nicol getting married and happily rearing a big family of children, while Robbie went off to the whaling and finally got command of his own ship at last.

In between voyages, however, he always came back to the island, and there he got himself quite a name for the stories he told of his adventures at sea. Not everyone believed these stories, of course, for Robbie's imagination had not grown less with the years. And so, when the death of Yarl Corbie finally set him free to tell the story of Finn Learson, he was quite bothered to find that not everyone believed this either.

"A thing like that," said some, "is just too strange to believe. And anyway, nobody can ever tell how much of Robbie Henderson's stories are true, and how much of them are made up."

"Aye, he's just like his Old Da in that," said other people; but Elspeth spoke up then, and told them,

"Robbie didn't make up the bit about Finn Learson's look. *I* remember what it was like. And I remember the way I felt it drawing me to the shore of the voe on that Up Helly Aa."

"I don't think he made up the bit about the Skuddler, either," Nicol remarked. "I remember how I fought Finn Learson that night, and how I seemed to have a power beyond my own strength. I remember, too, how that power seemed to go from me, as soon as I was below high-water mark."

"And Yarl Corbie *was* a wizard," Robbie reminded everyone; which made them all pause to think again, since no one had any doubts at all on that score.

There was one further thing which struck the people of Black Ness then. All of them had noticed a bull seal which haunted the voe from time to time —a huge, old fellow which had only one eye, and which had certainly never been known to come into the voe *before* the night of Finn Learson's disappearance from the island.

To some of them, at least, this seemed to prove *something*—indeed, there were those who went as far as saying that this creature could be the Great Selkie haunting the scene of the terrible revenge Yarl Corbie had taken on him. And as for Robbie himself, of course, he was quite convinced that this was the case.

In spite of all this, however, there were still people who believed that Finn Learson had been no more than the young man he had seemed to be. And so the argument went on, with these same people always claiming that Robbie was just telling the kind of story his Old Da used to tell, and that it would be foolish to think otherwise.

So a great many more years went by, until Robbie himself was an Old Da, with grandchildren who had never heard of the Selkie Folk until he spoke of them. Yet still, even after the passage of all these years, the one-eyed selkie continued to appear in the voe; and every now and then there would be some youngster who came asking Robbie questions about it.

To each and every one of these young folk, then, he told of the stranger who came ashore, exactly as that story has been given here; and it no longer bothered him if any of them said,

"I don't believe that!"

Robbie could remember himself saying the very same thing the first time *he* had been told about the Great Selkie. Also, he was more than old by that time. He was wise—very wise; and so he never tried to convince anyone against that person's will. Instead, he did exactly what his own Old Da had done. He just laughed, and went on with another story.